AT
RISK

ALSO BY
S.G. REDLING

AT RISK

S.G. REDLING

THOMAS & MERCER

Published by Thomas & Mercer, Seattle

www.apub.com

Amazon, the Amazon logo, and Thomas & Mercer are trademarks of Amazon.com, Inc., or its affiliates.

ISBN-13: 9781503939677
ISBN-10: 1503939677

Cover design by David Drummond

Printed in the United States of America

For unless Conscience knows
Truth, history is static.
See Hope itself tremble.

Written on a temporary art installation at Millory
Hall, St. Agatha's School for Girls, Ellicott City, MD,
1993–1995

Monday, October 5

She clung to the shelf support with one hand. She felt dampness on her aching knees but she didn't know if it was blood from where she'd scrambled around earlier or from the steel wire cutting into them. Maybe the blood from the wound on her side had started to run down her leg. Maybe it wasn't even her blood. It wasn't important. She wouldn't be kneeling here on this shelf long.

Her hands were dry and that's what mattered. She gripped the metal pipe, rotating her shoulder in the narrow space to be sure she had room to swing it when she needed to. It was just a matter of time until they found her. There wasn't that much space to search. She wondered which one of them would be coming through the door and then she figured that didn't matter much. What mattered was that they came after her hard and fast.

Colleen gripped the pipe and waited.

CHAPTER ONE

Wednesday, September 30

Wrong.

Something was wrong.

Colleen scanned the table. She should have offered to decorate the tables. After all, this was a fund-raiser for her husband's charity. Of course, if she had agreed to decorate, Colleen could only imagine the level of anxiety she would be feeling right now. As it was, she felt personally responsible for the spots on the water glasses, for the rock-hard butter, for the fact that the woman on the other side of Patrick was cutting her dinner roll instead of breaking it.

To her left, John sipped from his second—no, third—bourbon on the rocks. He'd slipped out twice to the bar as the room had settled at the tables. The club really shouldn't allow people, especially non-members, to buy drinks at the clubhouse bar and bring them into catered events. John's eyes were glassy and his lips looked wet. The bartender should know better. She should say something to John, or maybe to the bartender, but she knew she wouldn't. She knew she really shouldn't. Her instincts were not to be trusted.

Colleen caught herself. She always did this; she created disasters in her mind where none existed. Emotional compass set to Anxiety as true north with the sun always rising over Calamity. Head south to Catastrophe and ride on into the sunset of Failure and Shame. That was the Colleen McElroy way.

Everything was fine. She caught her fingers tracing the double strand of pearls around her neck, a comfort gesture. Maybe she shouldn't have worn this dress. Did the caramel color wash her out? She was almost forty; she had to start worrying about things like that. Maybe she should have worn the pink dress. But it was nearly October, really too late in the year for pink.

What was wrong with her?

"I'm nervous." The words were warm in her ear. Patrick, leaning in close to her, whispering. "It doesn't matter how many times I give this speech. I don't think I'll ever get used to speaking to crowds of people."

If Colleen's anxieties were exaggerated, Patrick's were delusional. Crowds loved hearing him speak. What was not to love? Her husband was the very definition of tall, dark, and handsome. Couple that with his soft, deep voice, carefully modulated to restrain the harder edges of his childhood accent, and Patrick McElroy made a nearly perfect public speaker. His passion for the topic sealed his fate as the charity spokesman most often invited to these civic organization fund-raisers.

At the head of the room, a large, tacky banner hung askew from the dropped ceiling. "B-BAD, Do Good." The Bluegrass Business Area Development committee dragged that worn banner out to cookouts and bike rallies and car washes. It looked out of place in the grand ballroom of the Shawnee Trace Country Club, but Colleen reminded herself that this was just one of a million things that she didn't need to worry about tonight.

Breathe. Relax. Be calm. Always be calm.

Colleen knew very few of the people sitting at the other tables. Shawnee Trace had never been a country club she had frequented, neither as a child nor during her first marriage. She remembered her first husband referring to it as one of the "country schlubs," his nickname for any of the newer establishments in the Lexington area that didn't cater to people of his pedigree. From what Patrick had told her, the attendees tonight were businesspeople like himself and John. Bank managers and insurance sales people and advertising executives who spent their time and their money on charitable events like this, both for the good of the community and the good of their personal networking.

Being a stranger here made Colleen relax a little. Nobody would give her any knowing looks. Hopefully nobody knew anything about her disastrous first marriage. Tonight she was the wife of Patrick McElroy and nothing else.

"Do I look okay?" Patrick whispered as a small woman in a blue suit made her way to the podium. "Is my tie on straight? Anything on my face? How do I look?"

Colleen turned to face him. She smiled and told the truth.

"You look perfect."

The little woman did the perfunctory microphone dance, tapping and blowing into it, wrestling the metal neck until feedback blasted out into the room. The crowd responded with the usual groans and laughter. As the woman introduced herself—president of some bank or something—Colleen wondered why nobody ever seemed to check the microphones out before evenings like this. She worried that Patrick might not be able to raise the microphone high enough, that not everyone would be able to hear him.

When another man, who looked like he had buttoned his coat over a beach ball, came to the podium to the applause of the room, another bolt of anxiety shot through Colleen. Had they introduced the wrong man? Or had she somehow told Patrick the wrong evening? Were they at the wrong event? If they were, it was surely her fault. She would have to apologize for all of them. To everyone. It would be so awkward and she would never be able to show her face here again.

Colleen recognized the train wreck she was driving herself toward. She was being insane, hysterical. Ridiculous. Stupid.

Breathe. Relax. Be calm. Always be calm.

Beach Ball Man said something Colleen missed and everyone applauded again. Patrick squeezed her hand and rose from the table. To her left, John rattled the ice in his otherwise empty glass.

"Go get 'em, partner," he said, toasting Patrick. John's wife, Bix, joined him in the salute, lifting her wineglass to Patrick and whistling loudly as he made his way to the podium. Colleen wondered how many glasses of wine Bix had had. She hoped the waiters would stay away during Patrick's speech. Judging by their slouched postures, neither Bix nor John needed any more to drink tonight.

Then Patrick moved behind the podium and Colleen felt something loosen within her. He adjusted the microphone easily, no feedback, no bumping. His large hands rested relaxed along the sides of the wooden stand. Patrick needed no note cards for this.

"Good evening. Thank you for being here tonight. My name is Patrick McElroy and I am one half of the Macaroni Brothers. And that slightly rumpled-looking fellow at my table"—he waved toward John—"is John Mulroney, the other half.

"Now, some of you might be wondering how two fine-looking Irishmen became the Macaroni Brothers. You might be wondering what a ragtag freight company has to do with the important work being done at Green Fields Youth Home. And some of you have heard this story so often you'd probably double your pledge just to keep me from telling it again."

A polite chuckle rippled across the room and quieted on cue as Patrick spoke again.

"Thirty years ago this Christmas I began my first of many stays at the Clark-Esler Home for Boys in Pikeville, Kentucky. I was nine and I was small for my age. My first night there, I got the stuffing beaten out of me by three older boys. My second night, there were five of them."

Patrick paused. "But on the third night, as I was hiding in my bunk, dreading the footsteps I knew would be coming for me, I found, wedged between the mattress and the frame, a Louisville Slugger with duct tape around the grip. I thought it was a miracle. I thought Santa Claus had finally found me in that dark, frightening place."

Even the waiters stood silently, enrapt by Patrick's soft, even tone.

"And when that door opened and those footsteps came near, I jumped out of bed swinging that bat like I was launching a grand slam in the World Series. All I could hear were footsteps running for the door and I kept swinging and swinging that bat." He shook his head. "I never did hit anything. The only damage I managed to do was to make myself so dizzy that I fell down and gave myself a shiner on the edge of the nightstand."

Only a few risked a hesitant laugh.

"And then I heard a voice," Patrick said. "This surprised me, because up to this point, the nine gentlemen I shared a room with had been noticeably silent during my initiations. But the lights came on and standing before me was a fat kid in a Duke T-shirt, missing both of his front teeth, grinning at me. He didn't look the least bit worried about the weapon in my hand or the black eye I had just given myself. He just grinned at me and said, 'Oh hey, you found my bat. Wondered where that'd got to.' Then he laughed and climbed back into his bunk. In that moment, I understood something very important."

Patrick leaned forward on the podium and every person in the room leaned in toward him.

"I understood that any kid tough enough to wear a Duke T-shirt in the great Commonwealth of Kentucky was the kind of kid I wanted in my corner."

Laughter, applause, and a few hoots and hollers rolled in. Patrick and John shared a look Colleen had seen many times before. It was a look that held a lot of history, good and bad.

"That fat kid was John Mulroney. We both went in and out of foster homes and back and forth to Clark-Esler, and we always found each other. As the years went by, people forgot which one was McElroy, which was Mulroney. McElroy, Mulroney. I guess it was inevitable that some comedy genius would come up with the Macaroni Brothers, and the name just stuck."

Patrick raised his glass of water and John raised his ice in unison to toast each other.

"We made a lot of plans over the years in Clark-Esler and we made a lot of promises to each other. One of those promises was to go into business for ourselves, and here we are, heading up the small"— he winked—"but aggressively growing Macaroni Brothers Freight Company."

He paused for polite applause.

"Another promise was that if we ever had the means—and we would do everything we could to acquire the means—we would build a home for kids like ourselves that was safe, clean, and afforded possibilities Clark-Esler and so many state-run homes cannot. We've kept that promise, too, with the building of Green Fields Youth Home."

More polite applause and John stood up, waving for attention. He managed to keep his ice mostly in his glass. "Uh, Pat, we also promised to become rock stars. Weren't we going to tour with Aerosmith? That gonna happen anytime soon?"

The crowd laughed and Patrick shook his head. "Okay then, two out of three ain't bad."

Colleen laughed as always at the old punch line. She also noticed that Bix didn't. Instead she rolled her eyes and emptied her wineglass.

Patrick continued. "When we imagined Green Fields, we imagined a home for kids like us, stuck in the foster care system, out of their homes for a variety of reasons. We wanted a residence that would do more than warehouse kids. We wanted a home that would nurture these kids, educate them, feed them body and soul. Seven years ago we didn't know how to make a home like that possible, but with your help and the help of so many talented and generous people, I'm happy to report that as of this summer, Green Fields has housed over two hundred and fifty kids. We've graduated one hundred and twenty-nine high school seniors and have procured funds and scholarships for ninety college students."

Patrick let his gaze move over the crowd as they applauded. Colleen knew that each audience member would feel as if he were looking directly at them.

When they'd quieted, he went on. "But our work is far from done. A study done in 2014 reported that over thirty thousand Kentucky children are homeless. Not all of them are in foster care and not all of them are without their families, but any child without a home is a child that is at risk. The kids that come to Green Fields are at risk. They are at risk of malnutrition, abuse, slowed or stopped education. The longer they are at risk, the higher their risks become."

He lowered his head and cleared his throat. When he looked back at the crowd, Colleen knew the emotion in his voice was not an affectation. "I was one of those kids. My partner, John Mulroney, was one of those kids. We know the risks. With your continuing generosity, we hope to continue minimizing those risks for hundreds more children so that they may become hopeful, educated, healthy adults with a future."

Of course the crowd rose to their feet. Who could resist? Colleen clapped so hard her hands grew hot and smiled so broadly her face hurt. Bix whistled some more and made a *whoop-whoop* sound while punching the air. John even put down his glass. Patrick's face warmed with a charming blush as he held up his hands, trying in vain to quiet the impressed crowd. Finally, the applause slowed, seats were retaken, and Patrick laughed.

"You sort of ruined my closing statements with that." Everyone laughed. "So I will step down now. Please stay for drinks and dancing. Take a good look at the plans for the new equine center that are posted in the lobby. Thank you for your time and your generosity. Now, if I haven't bored her to death, I'd like to ask my lovely wife, Colleen, to dance with me. Thank you, everyone."

More applause rose as people pushed back from their tables and headed to the dance floor at the far end of the room. Bars were set up on either side of a small jazz combo. Colleen waited for her husband as John and Bix made a beeline for the bar.

Colleen took Patrick's offered hand and let him lead her and the rest of the room onto the dance floor. It took several minutes to make it all the way across the room since it seemed everyone wanted to stop them, shake Patrick's hand, and congratulate him on the good work happening at Green Fields. Patrick never rushed anyone, taking the time to greet each of them by name, thanking them for their time and generosity. Sometimes he introduced Colleen. Several times she made a point of hanging back, giving him the moment for himself.

Finally, they made it to the floor and a slow, jazzy number started. Patrick held her hand and the small of her back, pulling her closer to his chest. She could feel the tension in his shoulders, could sense him calming himself down. He might make public speaking look easy, but Colleen knew how much pressure he put on himself.

"You were fabulous up there," she whispered to him, brushing her temple along his jawline. "You had them eating out of your hands. As always."

He laughed under his breath and led her in a turn. As she stepped past him, following his lead, his eyes moved over her from head to toe. His face looked serious.

"I wonder if you should have worn that dress."

Colleen didn't freeze or stumble, but something deep within her went rigid, all systems on alert. She felt her face heat up as a million critical voices went over her choices for her dress, hair, makeup, jewelry, shoes, perfume, toothpaste—

He pulled her back in close to him and his breath warmed her ear as he whispered, "You look so perfect nobody will believe we need the money."

She melted against him. Dancing with Patrick, she didn't need to repeat her mantra. Dancing with Patrick was better than breathing, relaxing, being calm. Always calm.

Patrick hummed along to the music, his large hand on the small of her back making her wish he would pull her even closer, inappropriately closer. No time for that. Even as he moved her smoothly across the floor, even as he squeezed her hand in his, he worked the room. Smiling, nodding, little words of greetings. Patrick knew how to work a room; he knew how to appeal to people. He remembered names and children and even the occasional pet. Bix often accused him of being a phony, a schmoozer, or a climber, but Patrick ignored her.

Green Fields meant everything to Patrick. She knew it meant a lot to John and to Bix, too, but Patrick's fire for the continuation of the home drove her husband to work long hours, stay up late nights, doing everything in his power to keep their vision alive. Every dollar of profit for the Macaroni Brothers meant more money for Green Fields. He obsessed about details with the staff—security for the children, the best nutrition, counseling, education, always looking for ways to safely expand to allow even more children into the residence and out of harm's way.

Patrick rarely talked about the specifics of his time in the state home, except when he and John told raucous stories about people with names like Booger and Fat Matt and No Nose Nelson. They laughed and exaggerated and made the years sound like one long adventure. Nowhere in the stories did they explain the many scars on Patrick's body, the clusters of cigarette burns on his feet and wrists, the unexplained compulsions to double-lock doors and keep stashes of food in odd places. And none of the stories they told together ever addressed any time before either boy had arrived at Clark-Esler.

Just the edges of those stories slipped out in the darkness, when it was just Colleen and Patrick in bed, naked and warm, in that private space that only opens when you've given yourself to another. He didn't offer much and she never pressed. Honestly, she wasn't sure she really wanted to know. The thought of anyone hurting her Patrick before he was the strong, disciplined, and passionate man he was now suggested a horror that she didn't want to let into her mind.

As it was, the kids of Green Fields broke her heart whenever she stopped by the campus—kids as young as twelve, as old as eighteen. Some of them were in trouble, some of them were escaping it. And then there were those kids who had no place to go and nobody to turn to. Those were the kids Green Fields went after. Those were the kids whose paperwork was expedited, whose medical records—if they had any—were transferred. Those kids got short-listed and welcomed to a clean, safe environment, maybe for the first time in their young lives.

It was so far from her own reality. Colleen and her sisters had grown up pampered and doted on. They enjoyed private schools and years abroad, with every opportunity afforded to them. Every kindness showered upon them by their parents. The world had been handed to each of them on the proverbial silver platter.

Of course, the problem with proverbial platters was that they had no room for reality. Colleen had gotten her big dose of reality served to her with fists and the heels of boots. She had gotten it punched into her and choked out of her by her first husband, a man raised in the same coddled way she had been. She had been blindsided by a cruel aspect of reality her soft upbringing had never prepared her for.

What had happened to Heath that had instilled such brutality into him? What about her had awakened his rage? They had seemed so similar at first glance, so suitably matched. Two well-born, well-educated, pampered children perfectly paired to slide into their parents' place in Lexington society. All logic said they should have lived out their lives in easy leisure, raising blond children like themselves who would have no more connection to the damaged children of Green Fields than the checks they would write at fund-raisers like this.

No, proverbial silver platters didn't do much good when it came time to serve up reality.

Colleen had scars of her own, scars she never imagined she would carry. While they might not compare to the ridges from burns and broken bones that marred Patrick's beautiful body, her scars brought with them ugly memories of their own.

Patrick turned her on the dance floor, his thumb rubbing warm circles on her back.

But all those scars brought with them were memories, she reminded herself. Memories came from the past. Patrick was her future. Tall, proud, passionate Patrick. Now she was part of the solution for hundreds of at risk children. Now Patrick was the anchor of her life.

Her future looked beautiful.

CHAPTER TWO

"Get out of the way."

Colleen laughed as John nudged his way in between them.

"Don't you have a date?" Patrick asked, surrendering his grip on Colleen.

"I think she's thrown me over for the bartender," John said, winking at Colleen. "I've seen his bourbon selection. It's probably a pretty good decision."

"So now you're just taking my wife?" Patrick laughed as John spun Colleen away from him. "Do I have any say in this?" he called after them. Colleen waved to him as John moved her across the floor.

Despite the Macaroni Brothers label, nobody ever believed that John Mulroney and Patrick McElroy were related by blood. Aside from their dark hair, they bore no resemblance to one another. Where Patrick stood tall and lean, John only aspired to six feet. His chubby cheeks and little potbelly hinted at a love of creature comforts over discipline and exercise.

He wasn't unattractive. On the contrary, Colleen had always considered her husband's partner to be surprisingly appealing. He was quick with a laugh and smile, even quicker with a compliment, and managed to deliver all of them with an open-faced sincerity that put Colleen at ease. John Mulroney was a man who enjoyed things—food, company, jokes, booze—and he did so with joyous abandon.

And truth be told, he was a much better dancer than Patrick.

The band began playing "Sentimental Journey" and John spun her again.

"Oh, I love this song." He hummed as he guided her through the other dancers, holding her close enough to lead, but never crossing the line to inappropriate. "It's so nice to dance with a woman who lets me lead for a change."

Colleen laughed. "Bix told me she's the one who taught you to dance."

"Of course she did. Bix thinks she taught Jesus how to walk on water. No, no, no, Colleen." Another spin. "My parents taught me to dance. They were lousy at a lot of things but they loved to dance. You're a pretty fine hoofer yourself, Mrs. McElroy."

"Thank you, Mr. Mulroney. I learned the same way you did. My parents loved to dance."

He lowered her into a gentle dip. "Really? Well now, here I thought you'd learned your fancy footwork in finishing school."

"Hardly." Colleen let him right her. "St. Agatha's was known more for field hockey than fox-trots. Besides, it was an all-girls school. Who were we going to dance with?"

John laughed that easy laugh of his. When the band broke into "I Left My Heart in San Francisco," he grinned at her expectantly. "Come on. We don't dance together enough at these things. One more." When she hesitated, not knowing if Patrick needed her, he pulled her close to him and whispered, "Now tell me the truth, Colleen. Just between you and me—I'm a better dancer than Patrick, aren't I?" Spin. "C'mon, tell me the truth."

Colleen laughed, scanning the room over John's shoulder for her husband. He stood by the bar, talking with the little woman who had introduced the evening. He looked busy, engaged. Always working. John turned to see what she was watching.

"Uh-huh," John whispered. "See? There's my proof. A good dancer would never waste time hustling for business when there's a beautiful woman waiting to dance with him."

"Watch it, John," Colleen said with mock-seriousness. "Talk like that will make your wife jealous and neither one of us wants that."

John laughed loudly. "No we don't want that." He pretended to duck out of sight of Bix, who stood in line for a drink. He whispered again. "But if she ever does get mad at you, remember what I told you to do. Call her Beatrice. That'll stop her in her tracks."

"I wouldn't dare. According to Patrick, you're the only person alive who can get away with calling her that."

He hummed in agreement. "Probably. But don't let her fool you. Beatrice has her soft side. She just hides it really, really well."

"Just like Patrick," Colleen said, following John's easy lead.

"Ah, yes. Patrick does have a soft side," John said. "And I believe you are the key to it, Miss Colleen. He does love you so very much. To be honest, I'm a little jealous. I used to be Pat's one and only." He winked and held Colleen out for a twirl.

When he pulled her back to him, John's eyes were soft and a little sad. Colleen didn't know how much of that was bourbon. He hummed along to the music, his hand warm on her back. There was no getting around it—he was a better dancer than her husband.

"You've got a good man in Patrick," he said softly. "I hope you know that."

"I do. I really do." Even Fred Astaire couldn't have made her forget that.

"He wants so much to impress you. All this work, all this building, it's not just for the kids. You know that, right?" He looked into Colleen's eyes as he spoke. "I mean, Green Fields is incredibly important to both of us and the business is growing, but since Pat met you, his focus is different. He wants to be a good man for you. He would do anything for you. You know that, right?"

Colleen felt her cheeks warm. She didn't know what to say. She couldn't help but feel that she didn't completely understand what John meant by this. It wasn't like John to get heavy when he was drinking. Sure, he occasionally got weepy and sentimental, lots of hugs for Patrick and "I love you, man" affirmations. But this? This felt different.

"He is a good man," she said. "Not just for me and certainly not because of me. In every way, Patrick is a good man because that's who he is."

He nodded. "He's come a long way. But you and I both know that story he tells at these things is a very sanitized version of what actually happened, right? That business with the bat, the big kids. Getting a black eye on the nightstand? We both know the story is a lot worse than that. Our boy has put some serious stuff behind him. We both have."

Colleen felt a familiar bewilderment. John and Bix and Patrick all spoke with a sort of cultural shorthand, assuming a knowledge of foster care that Colleen didn't possess. Of course the story was sanitized; she knew enough to understand that the true story was too violent for a dinner party speech. But how violent? Was there something she was supposed to understand, some unspoken wisdom she could never attain? Was he waiting for her to say something? He went on. "It can be hard to put the past behind you. It can stay with you, you know? Me and Pat, we both wanted out of there so much. And now here we are, professionals, raising money for kids like us. You'd think all that crap would be in the past, you know?"

Were those tears in John's eyes? She didn't get to be sure because he pulled her close to him, spinning with her easily across the floor. She thought he had wanted to lighten the mood. Then she heard him whisper in her ear.

"Patrick is a good man. Make sure you remember that. Both of you."

A loud bark of a laugh from across the room snapped Colleen from the moment. Bix's volume was rising. Colleen and John looked over at the bar to the left of the band. Judging from the tight, insincere smiles on the faces of those nearby, she was probably regaling that end of the room with a series of her legendarily filthy jokes.

Patrick was beside them in an instant, hissing into John's ear. "Get over there and get your wife under control."

John shook his head. "You know what will happen if I go over there. You know Bix. She's drunk. She'll start throwing punches."

Both men turned to Colleen.

"I'll get her," she said without enthusiasm.

Patrick whispered through gritted teeth, "Don't let her make a scene."

With a kiss to her temple, he urged her forward. Colleen cut through the crowd and heard John in a mock argument with an older gentleman, insisting he be allowed to cut in and dance with his lovely wife. He laughed loudly at something, no doubt trying to draw attention away from the scene at the bar.

As expected, Bix stood near the bar, letting a very drunk donor feel her up as she recounted some bawdy gossip, much to the horror of a well-dressed white-haired couple waiting for their drinks. Colleen smiled as she cut into the crowd and cut off Bix's story.

"Bix, how are you?" She made her smile and her tone bright. Why Patrick and John thought she was qualified to take on a drunk Bix was beyond her but she would do her best.

Patrick spoke up right behind her. "Mrs. Haley, Dr. Haley, how nice to see you again."

The only thing in the room stiffer than the woman's white hair was her rigid smile. Colleen felt a flush of relief knowing Patrick had waded into this mess with her.

"Hello, Patrick, nice to see you, too." Her voice was pure Bourbon Trail. "You and the development council have certainly brought together all the pieces of a wonderful event."

Colleen caught the dig—the event had all the pieces to be a success, but those pieces were not coming together, not while Bix was within earshot.

"That's very nice of you to say, Mrs. Haley. We certainly appreciate you being here. A worthwhile cause deserves—"

Bix cut him off with a drunken snort, throwing her arm around her drinking buddy's shoulders, which pressed her left breast higher onto his lapel. He took in the view and let Bix retake the floor. "So anyway, as I was saying, I told that old fool to head on down to the paddock. He'd find his wife straddling that stable boy. Told that dumbass he'd been paying stud fees to the wrong man." The pair cackled and smacked their tumblers together. If their drunk aim hadn't been off, they would have hit hard enough to shatter them. As it was, they managed to spill more of their liquor than they drank.

Bix peered at Colleen over her glass, then bumped her drinking buddy with her hip. She pretended to whisper, "I think I'm in trouble."

He kept his eyes on her breast as it came ever closer to escaping from her neckline. "I bet you get in trouble a lot. I bet you're all kinds of trouble."

Bix laughed but kept her eyes on Colleen, who stared back at her with an easy smile. Colleen knew better than to get aggressive with Bix, especially when she was drinking bourbon. Force wouldn't work. Patience might.

"Alright." Bix sighed and pulled away from the drunk man, making him stagger. Dr. Haley scowled at him and Mrs. Haley nodded at Colleen with prim approval. Bix put a whiskey-wet hand on Colleen's shoulder. "I need to powder my nose," she said with an exaggerated purr. "And I need to take a piss. Wanna go?"

"Let's." Colleen linked arms with Bix and held her steady while they made their way to the ladies' room. People greeted them as they passed, congratulating them on a wonderful evening, inviting the two women to join them in a toast. Bix smiled and laughed and called out to everyone who caught her eye. Colleen just smiled and kept them moving until she got her friend into the privacy of the ladies' lounge.

Bix burst through the door, throwing herself into the brightly lit powder room outside the bathroom proper. She squinted at the rows of lights over the makeup tables where several women sat touching up lipstick and hair.

"I have never understood," she said too loudly for the quiet room, "why the toilets need a lobby. Do you understand that, Colleen? Is that a rich people thing?"

So it was going to be that kind of night. In the mirrors, Colleen met the embarrassed glances of several of the women. As a group, they began to collect their belongings.

"Well now, don't everyone run off on my account!" Bix sat down heavily on the chintz couch in the corner. "I'm not gonna mess up anyone's hair. Y'all can stay."

The women filed out the door, the last to leave winking at Colleen and mouthing, "Good luck." Colleen nodded, pulling the door closed behind them.

"Don't lock it," Bix said, shouting toward the door that led to the bathroom. "There's still people in the toilets. We don't want to trap anyone who just snuck off to poop!"

"Bix, please." Colleen held up her hand—half stop sign, half surrender. Bix rolled her eyes again and crossed her legs, letting her shoe swing from her toe. A moment later, one toilet flushed, then another. Water ran and then two women hurried from the toilet room, brushing past Colleen without even a glance.

It seemed everyone in attendance knew Bix, at least by reputation.

Colleen gave a quick glance into the bathroom to be sure they were alone and then locked the powder room door. No doubt, word would spread why this restroom was busy.

When she turned back, Bix was no longer sprawled on the couch. Instead, she stood in front of the vanity pushing her thick, dark hair off of her face, trying to smooth out the cowlicks alcohol had awakened. Colleen moved to stand beside her. They watched each other in the mirror.

"You're like a little toy person," Bix said, squinting at their reflection. "Look at the size of you. What are you? A zero? A double zero? Where are your boobs?"

Colleen said nothing. Bix was larger than she in every way. Five inches taller, voluptuous in a way Colleen could never hope to obtain even with plastic surgery. Boobs, hips, ass, hair, makeup—everything about Bix demanded attention. She was all fullness and curves. Her sparkly clinging dress bordered on gaudy and her heels looked like they could nail a small animal to the ground. Even her teeth were larger than life—white and straight and perfect. Seeing her own pale blond reflection beside Bix's, Colleen felt like the same flat-chested wallflower she'd been in grade school.

Bix sighed. "I should've gotten another drink before we came in here."

Colleen blinked. "I'm not sure that would have been a good idea."

"Fuck, Colleen, if you're waiting for me to apologize, you can go ahead and sit your bony ass down because it's gonna be long, long time coming."

Blink. Wait. Colleen excelled at outwaiting drunks.

Bix sighed again. This time less dramatically. She turned her back to the mirror and leaned against the vanity. When she spoke again, her nasal twang lessened. She sounded tired.

"I hate these things."

"I know. I do, too."

"Yeah, but you"—she looked Colleen over—"you fit in. This is your thing, your people."

This again. While Bix could be a wild drunk, liquor tended to narrow her choice of topics. Like John and Patrick, Bix hailed from eastern Kentucky, coal country. Like them, she had plenty of tales of the foster system and hard times. She had actually met John when they were teenagers and both appearing in juvenile court.

When she and Patrick had started dating last summer, Bix and John had greeted her coolly at first, then began to welcome her with a careful politeness that led to some sarcastic jabs, especially from Bix. After the wedding in March, the situation had defaulted to an automatic foursome.

She and Bix had grown closer in the months since marrying Patrick. As different as they were from each other, they had found a rhythm, a shared space where they accepted each other. Bix grudgingly ceded to Colleen in matters of social decorum, knowing that the well-oiled wheels of Lexington society turned more smoothly for one of their own. And Colleen would never admit it to anyone but she admired the other woman's blunt dismissal of social propriety. Bix Mulroney truly didn't give a shit what anybody thought of her.

It was a revelation to Colleen. Especially after her first marriage. And the divorce. And the surgery. And the rest of it.

That was the real reason Colleen didn't lose her temper with Bix. Not because anger didn't work against her aggressive friend but because, as maddening as her social gaffes could be, in some weird way Colleen admired them. She might even envy them.

Patrick would never understand that. He expected Colleen to rub off on his partner's wife, for Bix to someday look at Colleen and say, "Oh my goodness, I feel like wearing plaid and espadrilles!" It was never going to happen. Bix would never change and Colleen would never expect her to. But it didn't mean her friend didn't exasperate her from time to time.

"Do you have any idea how much money we're hoping to raise tonight?"

Bix rolled her eyes. As many times as Colleen had seen her do that just this evening, it was a wonder Bix didn't get dizzy and pass out.

"I'm not doing anything to stop people from writing checks."

"You're acting like an ass."

"I'm acting like myself!" She stared as Colleen arched a pale eyebrow. She huffed. "Okay, maybe I am an ass but, god damn it, how come I have to be invisible at all these things? You'd think the Macaroni Brothers had been shot down from heaven by Jesus himself. Like they did all of this Green Fields shit on their own with no help from me. And who does Patrick mention in his little speech?"

She straightened her spine and dropped her voice into what Colleen assumed was supposed to be a lampoon of Patrick's soft tone. "'I'd like to thank my lovely wife, Colleen. Blah blah blah.' You think John would ever say shit like that? Hell no. Like I'm not good enough to even be here."

Her voice had grown louder and she jabbed her finger at Colleen's face. "Well, let me tell you something. I'm the kind of person these uptight fuckers are throwing their spare change at to save! I was one of those kids everyone is feeling so sorry for! We all were!"

Colleen said nothing, not wanting to fuel these fires she knew would keep popping up.

Bix liked to be shocking. Her volatile temper and mercurial mood shifts made her unpredictable. She liked to disrupt calm situations and watch the scandalized looks on people's faces. She had told Colleen once that when she was a kid, being outrageous was the only weapon she had and she still liked to wield it. She said it made her feel strong.

She didn't look strong. Not tonight.

Bix sat on the vanity, slumping so her hair tumbled forward around her face. She let it drape over her eyes and Colleen heard her breath catch.

Was Bix crying?

"Hey, no." Colleen stroked her bare arm. She hadn't realized Bix was drunk enough for tears. She only hoped tears meant Bix had put that sharp tongue away for the night. Colleen tried to make her tone sound comforting enough to cover the white lies she was about to speak.

"Bix, it's okay. People love you at these things. I know I'm supposed to tell you to sober up and act like a lady. Ugh. Act like me? Boring."

Bix snorted behind her hair and Colleen relaxed a little. "Everybody hates these events. Deep down, everyone is bored and they all secretly hope you'll dance naked on the bar or flip a table over or something. Even Patrick does, although he'd never admit it. Half the fun is that nobody ever knows what to expect when you're here."

She pushed Bix's hair back and raised her chin. Bix looked up from under wet lashes.

"Let's face it. The Macaroni Brothers' parties are nothing without you."

Bix's lips trembled, her eyes filling up. It was such an unusual sight Colleen could only watch fascinated as the tears shimmered on her lower lashes. She watched her swallow hard, watched her mouth work in hard spasms. Bix never had trouble finding the words to say exactly what she meant. Colleen didn't know what to expect.

The voice that came out from behind those red lips and big white teeth sounded young.

"John is cheating on me. He's going to leave me."

"What?" The word left Colleen in a whoosh. It couldn't be. That was impossible. As volatile as their relationship was, John and Bix were like peanut butter and jelly, bourbon and ice, biscuits and gravy. She had never seen a couple as intertwined, as passionate, as in tune with each other as John and Bix. She didn't even know them except as part of each other.

Bix pressed her face into her hands. It would make sense though, wouldn't it? It would explain the tension that she had felt growing over the past few weeks, the uptick in the fights and closed-door meetings. If John told Patrick his plans, Patrick would object.

Wouldn't he?

"Thank you for not telling me I'm crazy." Bix sniffled.

"Why would I say that?"

"Because I know it sounds like I'm making it up."

"Wait a minute. Wait a minute." Colleen settled on the vanity beside Bix. She grabbed her hand and squeezed. "Did John tell you he was leaving? What happened?"

"He didn't tell me. He didn't have to. I know." A wet sob hitched in her throat. "I know. I've known John more than half of my life and I know he's leaving. He's found somebody else."

"What are you talking about? John is crazy about you." She squeezed her hand harder.

Bix pulled her hand away. "No. He's running around at some hoity-toity country club on the other side of town. One of those old ones. I've seen the receipts. He's keeping it a secret but I know he's been going there, getting drunk with who knows who." She wiped her nose with the back of her hand. "You know the kind of women I'm talking about. Skinny little rich bitches."

Bix must have realized how that sounded because she peeked at Colleen from the corner of her eye. Colleen ignored the jab. She had to keep Bix calm.

"First of all, Bix, have you seen yourself?" She waved a hand over the gaudy dress. "Have you seen the way every man in this building has looked at you tonight?" Bix turned her head away but Colleen kept talking. "I know you and John are fighting. When aren't you fighting? But I also saw him checking out your ass when you went to the bar, just like he checks out your ass every single chance he gets."

Bix didn't look convinced. The idea of someone checking out her ass was probably as ordinary to her as someone blessing her after she sneezed. As a skinny girl with no ass to speak of, Colleen could only imagine that sort of attitude.

"John loves you. Sure, he probably drinks too much, but he loves you."

Bix shook her head, her gaze fixed on the patterned carpet. "He's leaving me. I know it. He's keeping secrets. The people he's been talking to . . ."

"Who?" Colleen asked softly. "Do you know who it is? Maybe it's business?"

"Have you met my husband? My husband? Not Saint Fucking Patrick. John doesn't work when he's actually at work. He sure as hell isn't working at two in the morning in some bar."

Colleen rubbed her hand. "It might not be what you think, Bix. John likes to drink. He and Patrick have both seemed stressed lately. Maybe he's blowing off steam."

"He used to let me blow off his steam. He hasn't touched me in days."

"Well, that sounds like stress, too."

"What are you? A fucking marriage counselor?" Bix's head snapped up in one of those weird Bix-shifts. "I've been with John longer than both of your fucking marriages combined. Getting a divorce doesn't make you a fucking expert. I know how marriage works."

Colleen didn't get a chance to defend herself. Bix shook her head and shut her eyes. Her voice dropped to a resigned tone. "But yeah. Maybe it's nothing. Maybe we're just going through a rough patch."

She didn't sound very convinced but Colleen had no desire to question her. Instead she rubbed her back in what she hoped was a soothing manner. Bix stared straight ahead, a small flood rising in her eyes.

"I'm not like you, Colleen. I don't have another marriage in me. There isn't a Patrick waiting to pick me up and make my happily-ever-after come true." She turned to look into Colleen's eyes, her face the picture of misery. In that expression, Colleen could imagine the lost young girl she had been all those years ago. "I gave that man everything. I don't know who I am without John."

CHAPTER THREE

It looked like John had been poured into the back seat of Colleen's Camry by Patrick, who stood rigid with anger beside the car. She had heard angry words growled between the two men as she'd gotten closer but hadn't been able to make them out over Bix's drunken laughter. Colleen dumped Bix beside her husband with as much gentleness as she could manage.

"I got it. I got it." Bix hauled her feet into the car and yanked the door shut, nearly taking off Colleen's shoulder.

Patrick's lips were as white as his knuckles as he guided the car out of the country club parking lot. Bix and John muttered under their breaths and settled into the back seat. Colleen shot them a warning glance. She could feel the anger pulsing off of Patrick. If Bix and John began fighting, she couldn't guarantee Patrick wouldn't throw them both out of the car on the side of the highway.

Of course, Bix had to speak up first.

"Well, that was fun." She saw the daggers Patrick threw at her in the rearview mirror. "What? It was fun. Though the food was shit. Someone needs to teach them how to cook chicken. Mine is a thousand times better, and I never would have used that lame-ass canned corn.

Colleen, did you eat that chicken? Ugh." She snorted. "What am I saying? Colleen doesn't eat in public. It's vulgar." She dragged that last word out, approximating some sort of accent Colleen didn't bother to try to identify. "She probably just ate half a piece of celery and saved the rest for later."

John snickered. Whatever was wrong between them, it seemed Patrick's anger had convinced them to put it aside for the ride home. The two of them tried a few more slurred conversational gambits that fell on deaf ears before slouching down together to giggle in the seat for the duration of the ride home.

Patrick said nothing. He didn't look back at Bix or John again or acknowledge them in any way. Beside him, Colleen could see the muscles in his jaw twitching, a vein along his temple throbbing in tandem. She couldn't have spoken if she'd wanted to.

When they pulled into the Mulroneys' driveway, once again Bix spoke first. She threw open the door, then changed course, draping herself between the front seats and purring, "Thanks for a wonderful evening. Let's do it again real soon." Patrick didn't move when she planted a wet kiss on his cheek. Bix was still laughing as she made her way up the driveway to the front door.

John took longer to get out of the car. He thanked Colleen for a lovely evening without any of his wife's sarcasm. With a groan and a huff, he hauled himself out of the car, steadying himself on the door before closing it gently. Patrick put the car in reverse but stopped when John tapped on the glass.

For a moment, Colleen feared Patrick wouldn't roll down the window, that whatever had happened tonight—and clearly, this was more than Patrick just being embarrassed by Bix's drinking—had driven a lasting wedge between the two friends. They had been acting so strange lately, arguing and slamming doors. And then John had said such odd and serious things to her while they danced. John tapped again, no sense of urgency, confident his friend would roll down the window to hear him out. Patrick did just that.

But John didn't say anything.

Instead, he set both hands on the window frame, lowering his head to stare face to face at Patrick. Colleen couldn't see her husband's face but John's expression was not what she expected. There was no apology, no anger, no trying to laugh it off. It looked expectant. It looked like he had just asked Patrick a question, although Colleen had heard nothing.

They stayed that way for several moments, John's friendly, open face waiting for an answer to a question he never asked, Patrick still and silent but not looking away. Colleen didn't know what to do. Were they fighting? Should she say something?

Whatever silent discussion they'd been having came to an end. Patrick huffed an angry breath and looked away, shaking his head. John also shook his head, although he looked more disappointed than angry. He straightened up and tapped his hands on the car door. Colleen thought that was it, that he would turn and follow Bix inside.

Patrick apparently thought the same thing. He put the car into reverse and started to back up. John stopped him by leaning his head through the window once more.

"We're brothers, man. Don't you forget that."

Patrick stared at him. "I might say the same thing to you."

"I've got this under control."

Patrick looked him over from head to toe. "You don't have shit under control."

John stayed in the driveway, watching as they backed out and drove into the night.

• • • • • • • • • • • • • • • • • •

The drive home did little to cool Patrick's temper. Neither spoke the entire ride. They remained silent as Patrick unlocked the front door.

Normally, after an evening out, they would head to the kitchen for coffee or iced tea to talk about the night's events. Not tonight.

Colleen smelled bourbon.

Patrick was no drunk. At most, she had seen him whiskey-warm, his laughter a little looser, his cheeks a little flushed. He had never gotten messy. He had never gotten loud. He had never raised a hand to her in any way except loving. Tonight was no exception. She had seen him nursing a few drinks all night long, just to be social.

But the smell, that unique combination of bourbon and anger on a man, shot through any thoughts Colleen might have had and changed everything to fear.

Patrick McElroy had never directed his anger toward her. But she knew what real anger looked like. She knew how much it could hurt. She had the scars to prove it. It wasn't fair to him but the specter of her first husband haunted their marriage. So she stayed silent as they went upstairs to the bedroom.

When Colleen came out of the bathroom, Patrick headed in. He had finally begun to vent his irritation while she was out of earshot.

". . . and she keeps running her big, fat mouth. God, you could hear her in the lobby." He slammed the door of the medicine chest and talked over running water. "Both of them acting like idiots, like ten-year-olds with their first beer."

She could hardly make out the words as he talked while brushing his teeth—something about responsibility and building the business and doing it all on his own. She didn't ask him to repeat himself. She had heard versions of all of it before. Patrick wanted John more involved in the business. He wanted Bix to learn how to handle herself like a professional. He wanted both of them to get their acts together.

She listened for any indication Patrick knew John and Bix were having trouble. As irritated as he could get with both of them, how would he respond to them splitting up? He showed no signs of knowing anything about it as his rant tapered off.

Although this was the angriest Colleen had ever seen Patrick over John and Bix's behavior, it wasn't the first time she'd heard these complaints. She knew what to do.

When he began to cool down, she did what she always did. She started to detail all the evening's plus sides, all the positive feedback and the generous donations. She recited the compliments the plans for the equine center had received and recounted the wonderful impressions the three new employees had made on the guests. Colleen made sure to name names: Clairmont, Haley, Fulks, Berlinger—the guests he had introduced her to, the guests whose approval she knew her husband yearned for.

He listened to her as he hung up his suit and shook out his shirt before laying it into the laundry basket. He brushed off his shoes and rolled his belt so carefully. He did these things without thinking and Colleen watched him as she recounted for him all of the positive reports of the evening.

And when he came into their bed, smelling like mint and soap, she was reminded that Patrick still didn't take things like a clean house and expensive clothes for granted. He was still waiting for a bouncer or a cop or a social worker to remove him from this fine setting and take him back to whatever chaos he had come from. Most people didn't see that side of Patrick McElroy.

Colleen pulled the covers around them and made sure he knew he belonged.

CHAPTER FOUR

Thursday, October 1

"Are you eating my scones?"

Patrick spun around, trying to hide the mouthful of pastry. The crumbs on his lips negated the effort. He tried not to laugh while he tried not to chew and Colleen pretended to strangle him.

"These are for the kids! You are literally stealing food from foster children."

Patrick's laughter broke free, spraying them both with crumbs. She shouldered past him to grab the tray of scones but didn't resist when he pulled her back against his chest. She could smell lemon and sugar as he nuzzled her neck. He wore only his boxers and the heat of his bare skin burned through her thin pajamas.

Patrick McElroy half-naked eating scones in her kitchen was something Colleen didn't think she'd ever get enough of. The length of his body flush against hers, the thick muscles of his forearms crossed beneath her breasts would have kept her there forever. She sighed as his lips played over the sensitive spot below her ear.

"Nice try," she whispered. "You're not getting any more scones."

He laughed and held up the half scone he'd left on the counter. "I've got to finish this one. I can't give the kids half-eaten food. It's a health code violation." Colleen pulled out foil to wrap the plate of pastries. "You know, before I met you, I had never had a scone. I don't know if I'd even heard of them before. Now they're my favorite. What did you say they are? German?"

"English," Colleen said, watching him dunk a corner of the scone into his coffee. "Or Irish. I don't know. Something from the British Isles."

"Wherever they're from, the ones from Lexington are my favorite."

She curtsied at the compliment and pushed the wrapped tray aside. She'd been up since five making pastries and fresh fruit salad for the field trip today. Bix had told her to bring breakfast-type food; she'd take care of the heartier stuff. Since lemon was Patrick's favorite flavor, she'd made lemon cranberry scones and lemon bars. She started organizing the plates and bowls and serving utensils when she realized Patrick was just standing there, watching her.

"Am I forgetting something?" Defensiveness came by habit.

He shook his head. He leaned against the sink, his back to the window. The morning sun poured in around him, shining off the broad lines of his shoulders, diffused through his sleep-mussed hair. His large, scarred hands dwarfed the coffee cup and Colleen felt a strong urge to trail her fingers over the map of muscles beneath his skin. When he turned his head, the sun caught the tips of his long, almost feminine eyelashes.

"I'm sorry about last night."

The light playing over the lines of his face made it hard for her to remember last night, at least anything he needed to apologize for.

"I shouldn't have raised my voice."

She moved close to him, close enough to kiss the hard ridge where his collarbones met. This beautiful man thought he needed to ask forgiveness for raising his voice, for nothing more than a harsh tone, an ugly sound. She heard his coffee cup scrape against the counter and then felt his arms close around her again. A familiar dizziness washed over her. A year and a half after the divorce, almost seven months of marriage and she still hadn't found her equilibrium in the safety of Patrick. She could still be disarmed by his gentleness.

"You have nothing to apologize for."

"I do." He whispered into her hair. "I yelled. I ranted. I lost my temper." He sighed and kissed the side of her head. "I was just nervous last night. All those people. And then John. And then Bix. Oh my god, her mouth. And why does she always have to get so hammered?"

Colleen had no answer for that so she veered the subject away. "You and John have been fighting a lot lately." Patrick sighed. "Is it anything you want to talk about? Something to do with the business?"

He shook his head. "It's something we have to work out between us. It's nothing for you to worry about."

"But I do worry. I worry when I see you worry. You've been really tense lately." She smoothed her hands along his back. "Is it about money?" She heard his breath catch and hurried to add, "Because if it is, you know you can come to me."

"Colleen."

"You don't have to do everything alone. We're partners, aren't we?"

He pushed away and picked up his coffee. "I have a business partner. And I have enough on my plate keeping that from blowing up. I don't need to worry about handling you, too." He looked up at that and softened his tone. "I'm sorry. I didn't mean that the way it sounded."

Colleen nodded, unconvinced.

"Look, babe, you came through for me with the loan for the plane. You literally saved our business. I can never fully repay you for that."

"But you did," she said. "You paid me back every penny even though I told you there was no deadline for it at all."

"I wasn't talking about the money. I was talking about your generosity, your trust. You didn't question me about the money. You didn't doubt me. You just gave it to me. I can't tell you how much that meant to me."

Colleen swept invisible crumbs from the countertop. "It sounds to me like it means you don't trust me now, like somehow the fact that I lent you that money changed something between us. Closed some kind of door."

"No."

"No? Then how come you can't tell me what's going on? How come you don't talk about business with me anymore? You used to tell me everything—your plans for expansion, your new contacts, your marketing ideas. Now the only way I hear anything is when we get together with John and Bix and Bix tells me."

"I thought that stuff bored you. Business and all that."

"Bix knows all about the business." Colleen didn't know exactly why but his statement had stung, like an insult or a public humiliation. She hoped she didn't sound as petty as she felt.

"Bix works there. Part time, at least. And she helped us get it going."

Colleen nodded again, feeling small. "So I guess she used the last guest pass to the boys' club, is that it?"

Patrick dropped his head back and sighed to the ceiling. "That's not it. That isn't it at all. And surely by now you've learned how Bix is. She doesn't know as much as she thinks she does. The business has a lot of moving parts. She thinks because she answers the phone once in a while or signs for an order that she's the plant supervisor."

"She helped you all get Green Fields started. She told me that you couldn't have done it without her, that she's the only reason the funding came through."

"Do you believe that?"

Colleen shrugged. "How should I know? I only hear Bix's side."

"That's because nobody on earth can talk louder than her."

He winked at her, but Colleen wasn't in the mood to let this go.

"She was upset you didn't mention her last night from the podium. She says you never mention her when you do these fund-raisers."

Patrick nodded in surrender. "That's probably true. I probably should. She did wade through all the government paperwork. That's one upside to her relentless mouth—even the government bureaucracy can't shut her up. I think they gave us the funding and expedited the paperwork just to get her off the phone."

That made Colleen smile.

"But don't believe what she says about her being the heart and soul of Macaroni Brothers. John and I are the ones who hauled the boxes and fixed the trucks and lived on air sandwiches until we got our feet under us." Patrick shook his head again, as if the whole topic bewildered him. "John drives me crazy. If he spent a tenth of the time he spends boozing and chasing ass on building the business, we'd be bigger than FedEx. But he's put as much sweat equity into this business as I have."

"So what are you two fighting about?"

Patrick sighed. "The same thing you and I fight about. Taking work from Gables Medical Center."

"John thinks it's a bad idea, too?"

"John just doesn't like to work. John thinks we ought to just sit on our asses at the track and hope money falls into our laps. That stupid son of a bitch has no idea how—" He stopped himself and took a deep breath. It seemed he wasn't in the mood to have this particular discussion again either.

Colleen changed the subject. "Bix thinks John is cheating on her. That's why she was so upset last night. She thinks he's running around on her. I know he's a huge flirt but do you think he's actually cheating on her?"

"Honestly? Probably. It wouldn't be the first time. Not even close. Don't look at me like that." He downed the rest of his coffee. "It's complicated. John can be a mess and Bix is—well, Bix can be a lot to deal with. You know that. In their own way, they're perfect for each other."

"Do you even like Bix?"

"Yes, I do. I do." He sounded like he was arguing with himself. "I've known her a long time. She gets us, you know? She's funny and she's tough. It's just that she gets under my skin. She gets bossy, gets that tone of voice." He growled a frustrated sound, then shook his head. "But the truth is she's smarter than she looks."

Colleen nodded. "She'd have to be, wouldn't she?"

She held her breath as Patrick snapped to attention at that. Would he take offense? Get mad? She exhaled when she saw him start to chuckle.

"I guess she would."

Down went the coffee cup and up came the arms, inviting Colleen into her favorite place to rest. She let him pull her close and breathed in the warmth of his skin.

"None of this matters, Colleen. What's going on with John and her is their business. What's between me and John is between us. It has nothing to do with you and I shouldn't have taken it out on you last night."

"If it affects you, it affects me."

He smoothed his hands along her back. "Your happiness affects me more than John's crap, more than Bix's big mouth. Making you happy is what matters to me. You are the best thing that ever happened to me, Colleen." She closed her eyes as he put his lips to her forehead. He whispered into her skin. "Well, you and those scones."

CHAPTER FIVE

It didn't take long to make it to the hangar. Despite the size of the University of Kentucky and the many medical and industrial centers that surrounded it, Lexington proper did not take up a lot of land. From their house just north of the historic district to the Medoc Industrial Park that was home to the Macaroni Brothers Freight Company, they could circumvent downtown traffic by taking New Circle Road, the city's beltway. Medoc was one of a half dozen industrial parks with private runways operating under the watch of the Blue Grass Airport several miles west.

Even though she had grown up in Lexington, the long stretches of warehouses were unknown territory for Colleen. She was no stranger to private planes and had even seen a few private runways on the larger estates that ringed the edges of the city, stretching from Georgetown to Jessamine County, but Macaroni Brothers' space was no country estate, and the Medoc Industrial Park was more blacktop than bluegrass. Still, Colleen knew how proud Patrick was of the enormous gray hangar. She saw that little smile on his face at the sight of the Macaroni Brothers sign.

Patrick drove past the office in front, the only room in the metal building with a window, and parked on the right side between two other Macaroni Brothers trucks. A service road ran behind the length of the industrial park with painted lanes leading to the runway twenty yards out. Patrick and Colleen unloaded the food and brought it to the rear of the hangar, where both truck bay doors and the enormous plane bay door stood open.

On the edge of the road closest to the hangar, between the open bays, Bix stood fanning a barbecue grill, smoke billowing up around her. She waved them toward the truck bays with a grill fork.

"I've got the tables set up for the picnic," she yelled. "Put the cold stuff at the end. I'm going to put the hot dishes on the Sterno." Colleen waved back, then set about stacking the trays of pastries in her arms. Patrick grabbed the fruit salad and followed her.

It seemed a strange place for a picnic. Even the service road with its rumbling trucks might have been a better choice. The hangar smelled of oil and rubber. At this end, a maze of racks and shelves and pallets left little room for the wobbly table Bix had set up.

"Maybe we should move this over to the other end of the building," Colleen said to Patrick—in a whisper, lest Bix hear her decisions being questioned. "It's filthy down here."

Patrick shrugged. "I'm sure she has her reasons. And I can't say I mind not having food too close to the Cessna."

So Colleen dropped the subject. When the wind shifted and blew charcoal smoke into the hangar, however, she wondered about the wisdom of this entire endeavor. She scowled at a squat, square-looking truck parked against the wall between the plane doors and the truck doors, with only the metal wall of the hangar between it and Bix's flaming grill. Colleen didn't know much about the hangar or the sea of gear and equipment housed within it, but even she understood the words "Fuel Truck." But she seemed the only one concerned about it, so she kept her mouth shut and unloaded the food.

Bix hadn't skimped, as usual. A half dozen big foil pans cluttered the table, leaving Colleen little room for her own contribution.

"Hold on! Hold on!" Bix ran in, waving the fork like a baton. "Let me get that out of the way. I brought enough food to feed an army and I only had a chance to set up one table." She started shoving containers around, making a commotion out of the project. Behind her, holding the fruit salad, Patrick sighed.

"They're not being sent to a desert island, Bix," he said. "They're going to have eaten breakfast before they get here. And then they're going to get dinner when they get back. The food is good at Green Fields. We're just giving them a picnic, not trying to keep them alive for the winter."

"Shut up, Pat. I like feeding them." She took the bowl from Patrick and held his gaze. "Are we cool, Pat? After last night?" It took a moment, but Patrick nodded. Bix chuckled. "Attaboy. What did you bring, Coll?"

Colleen pulled back the foil on the two trays. Bix wrinkled her face in confusion.

"What are those? Biscuits?"

"Scones. They're lemon scones. And these are lemon bars."

"Oh. That's nice. I'm sure they're going to love those." She didn't do much to hide her sarcasm.

Colleen felt her face warm. "You said to bring breakfast."

"Oh my lord, Colleen, I'm just kidding!" Bix patted Colleen's back almost hard enough to hurt. "I'm so sorry. I wouldn't know a scone if it bit my big fat ass." Her voice was softer now, with none of her usual edge. "I'm serious. I didn't mean that to sound so shitty. You know me. I get wound up until I'm running around like a damn fool. I love feeding these kids."

"I know," Colleen said, feeling stupid for being so sensitive. "This is going to be fun. Patrick is dying to show them the new plane."

"Oh lord, John's like a five-year-old going to a bouncy house. I swear sometimes I wonder if they miss living in group."

They began arranging the table. Besides the pastries, there were hamburgers and hot dogs, baked beans, a sad-looking green salad, chips, and what Colleen knew was Bix's signature dish—fried corn. Bix served it every time they had dinner at their house, bragging about how much everyone loved it. To Colleen it tasted like frozen corn soaked in watery butter but Patrick and John both packed it away so she kept her opinions to herself. Like their love of baked steak and their insistence upon putting black pepper on absolutely everything, Colleen figured it was a taste acquired in childhood.

John wandered over to the table, whistling. "Hey, Colleen, Pat's raving about those lemon things you brought. Where are they? I want to get one before the savages devour everything on the table." She handed him one on a napkin and he bit into it with comical gusto. He clutched his chest like she knew he would. One thing about John, he loved food.

"These are amazing!" He sprayed crumbs as he spoke. "You gotta teach Bix to make these things."

"Shit," Bix laughed. "You think I'm spending my time squeezing organic lemons and creaming grass-fed butter or whatever other Martha Stewart Pinterest shit goes into those things, you are dreaming, John."

"They're not that complicated," Colleen said, yearning to change the subject. Bix took a lot of pride in her cooking and, if what she said last night was true, things between John and Bix were bad enough without making Bix defensive about her cooking. And to be honest, there weren't many things Colleen knew how to cook—her pastries were her only offerings when it came to potluck. She didn't particularly want to share the recipe with Bix.

What was wrong with her? Colleen felt her face redden again. Was this some kind of fifties' sitcom? Women fighting over pastry recipes?

"I'm thinking volleyball," John said. They were discussing activities for the kids' visit.

"Maybe Frisbee golf," Bix offered. "Or kickball. I used to kill at kickball."

"I used to play softball. Fast pitch," Colleen offered. Bix and John looked at her as if she had just said something impossible. "Believe it or not, yeah. I was the pitcher. We were pretty good, too. We won the club title three years in a row." John whistled and applauded as Colleen took a little bow.

Bix laughed. "Shit, we didn't have softball. It was hardball in the dirt. I spent my summers with my mamaw in Williamson and I was the only girl in the holler. I had to play with the boys and I learned real fast they didn't give a shit if I was a girl."

John cut her off with a pat on the ass. "Yes, Beatrice. We all know about your summers with your mamaw."

Bix glared at him. "I'm just saying that if I wanted to play, I had to play like they did. By the time I was thirteen, I was bigger than half of them. I could run . . ."

When Bix had her back turned, telling her story as she loaded up a tray from the grill, John winked at Colleen and rolled his eyes at his wife, flapping his fingers together like a puppet mouth and wiggling his hips in a pretty accurate depiction of Bix's walk. Colleen laughed without making a sound.

The Green Fields bus pulled around the building and Colleen hoped Bix had more to say. If Bix kept talking, that would spare Colleen the awkwardness she often felt around the kids.

She couldn't admit it, not even to Patrick, but she never knew how to act around the Green Fields kids. It didn't matter if they were young and wide-eyed, throwing their arms around anyone who would hug them back, or the tougher kids with their smirks and worldly boredom. Colleen always felt like she was saying the wrong thing. She felt shrill in their presence, prissy and uptight.

She felt guilty.

It wasn't her fault they found themselves in foster care. She knew that. But she felt a deep, almost primal guilt that these kids lived in a world she knew nothing about. Her husband had lived there as well

45

as John and Bix and all three of them moved among the kids easily, comfortably. Patrick had told her that the kids liked her, most of them at least. Especially the young girls. They liked her soft sweaters and her pearls. They liked her soft voice and the way she smiled. When Colleen told Patrick that they liked Bix better, that the other woman was better with the kids, he had shaken his head.

"She's not better with them. Most of them are just used to someone like her."

Whatever that meant, Colleen was glad for Bix and her over-the-top greeting for the kids. Two counselors from Green Fields, Colleen thought their names were Mandy and Ginny, guided them toward the hangar, toward the food. As predicted, Patrick hurried to tell them about the plane the Macaroni Brothers had purchased. John promised them all a chance at operating the small freight scale and Bix immediately started plating food.

Colleen stayed back, quiet, trying not to act like the old nuns at her mother's church, those silent stone women tucked into robes who simply nodded and smiled, occasionally patting a slow child on the head or hissing disapproval at someone acting out in the sanctuary.

This wasn't her scene. The hangar, the machinery, the kids—none of it felt natural to Colleen. This business was Patrick's dream; John's, too. Having these at risk kids here, knowing that their business played a part in their safety and development, meant everything to them. Colleen wanted to celebrate that. She wanted to be a part of it. For the life of her, she just didn't know how.

The more awkward she felt, the tenser and prissier she felt. The tenser she felt, the harder it became to speak, and forever onward. So Colleen stayed behind the food table and smiled like a nun.

Fortunately, her conversational skills weren't required beyond offering plastic utensils and scooping out food. Most of the kids ate the fried corn like they'd been waiting for it their entire lives. And Bix had properly anticipated the urge for black pepper with a new set of plastic salt and pepper shakers. The little packets in with the utensils would never be enough. The girls ate as much as the boys, piling up their plates between Patrick's and John's demonstrations.

This was only the second time Colleen had been in the newly expanded space. A month after Patrick had repaid Colleen for the loan for the plane, business had picked up sufficiently to move the plane from the small rented T-hangar and he put out a down payment for this larger, empty space at the industrial park.

They didn't need the whole space yet, Patrick had explained to her, but hopefully within the next three years, they would. John would be getting his pilot's license so both he and Patrick could fly runs for the medical center and other clients; they would soon be able to move their three drivers from part time to full time with benefits, maybe buy another plane. Because of the money the Gables jobs were bringing in, Macaroni Brothers Freight Company had the potential to go from running small freight and odd jobs locally to operating nationwide.

As she stood on an oil stain with Bix, dishing out food to foster kids from Green Fields inside of the cavernous, dirty building, her husband's dreams of grandeur seemed a bit premature, but Colleen had faith in Patrick and Patrick had faith in the business.

* * * * * * * * * * * * * * * * * * *

"Hey, Ziggy!" Bix pushed past Colleen to get around the table to hug the young woman who'd greeted them. She was short, with curly black hair tamed down into two thick braids that framed her dark, freckled face. The girl let Bix wrap her up in a full body hug. "You eat?"

"I did," Ziggy said, disentangling herself. "Now dessert. What flavor are these?" She pointed to the scones.

Bix put her arm around the girl's shoulder, smiling at Colleen like she was doing her a favor. "Those are scones. Mrs. McElroy made them. They're like biscuits."

"I know what they are," Ziggy said with a tone only a teenager could truly master. "They sell them at Starbucks. What flavor are they?"

"Lemon cranberry."

Ziggy brightened at that and grabbed one. "I was afraid they were pumpkin spice. Everything is pumpkin spice right now. I hate pumpkin."

Bix snorted. "White girl flavor, huh?"

Colleen's mouth dropped open but Ziggy just nodded. "My mom's white but I guess I didn't get her pumpkin genes." She spoke around a mouthful. "This is really good, Mrs. McElroy. Your stuff, too, Mrs. Mulroney."

"Oh shit," Bix said, slapping the girl on the arm. "Since when do you call me Mrs. Mulroney? I'm Bix to everyone."

Ziggy tilted her head in the direction of Mandy and Ginny, the counselors from Green Fields.

Bix nodded.

"Gotta play by the rules while the law is around, huh?"

The girl nodded. Green Fields kept strict rules for the kids—schedules and protocols, manners included. If the kids wanted to be eligible for field trips and events like this picnic, they needed to follow the rules. Colleen knew Ziggy had a reputation for breaking them.

Bix seemed to read her mind. "So if you're here today, it must mean you're staying in line. That's good, Ziggy."

The girl nodded, concentrating hard on the half-eaten scone. "I got mandatory drug testing. The judge said I had to pass for six months after the last time I went AWOL. He said if I could stay out of trouble for six months, he'd let me talk to him about getting emancipated when I turn sixteen."

"I hope you're going to stay in school," Bix said. Ziggy shrugged. "Because let me tell you something. You think it's tough going through the system? You think your social worker is on your back? Wait until you have a landlord. And a boss. And a phone bill to pay."

When this just earned another shrug, Bix moved her bulk in tight to the girl until she had to look straight up at her.

"You best think, and I mean *really* think," she said, her voice low now, just shy of menacing. "You drop out at sixteen, you'll be lucky to get a job at Burger King. And even if you get two shit jobs, you'll be lucky to keep a roof over your head, and you know where that leads. It leads back to the street and back to some piece of shit pimp or dealer, and then you're gonna look up and you'll be thirty going on a hundred and you'll wish you were dead."

Colleen saw Ziggy blink back tears. Now Bix took a half step away and rubbed the girl's back.

"Yo, Zig!" John called as he walked up to them. "We don't have all day, girl. Get your food and get your butt back over here and see all this cool stuff we've got."

Ziggy looked to Bix for permission, and Bix granted it with a wave. When they'd watched her join the group of girls following Patrick around the fuel truck, John turned to Bix.

"Come on, don't lecture her. They're here for some fun."

"Yeah, well she's not going to be having much fun when she winds up back in court and back in detention. Or worse, back on the streets giving blow jobs for a dollar a holler."

John rolled his eyes. "Lighten up, will you? She's having a little fun. Besides, she's got social workers all over her telling her that stuff all day long. She doesn't need it from you. You remember how it is, baby." He winked at her. "She's young. Let her have a little fun. Alright?" Bix nodded and he grinned. "That's my girl. Hey, make sure you save me some of that corn, okay, baby? Love ya."

Bix waved him off to join the kids examining the freight scale. She came back around the table to stand beside Colleen.

"These god damn kids. Break your heart every single day."

"You're good with them."

"I've been one of them," she said. "And I know John's right. These kids have got advice coming at them from every direction, especially at Green Fields. There's so damn many rules there they need their own constitution. But even with all those rules and all those counselors, they still fuck up. It's like a biological imperative at that age." She sighed. "You're young. You're beautiful. You think you're bulletproof. These kids have got this amazing facility at Green Fields, everything they need to be safe, and they're still sneaking out and running off to do drugs and god knows what else. And then there's John, Mr. Feel Good, telling me to lighten up."

"Did you guys make up last night?" Colleen asked. "Did you talk to him about what you told me? About his running around?"

Bix looked down at her and grimaced. "I was kind of a mess last night, wasn't I?" She didn't wait for Colleen to confirm it. "I was pretty hammered. I shouldn't drink bourbon in public. And I don't remember exactly what I said to you, but I remember it being kind of shitty, whatever I said about your divorce."

"Everything said about my divorce is shitty," Colleen said. "It's unavoidable."

Bix laughed. "Yeah but I didn't have to be mean to you about it. I get mad. I run my mouth. I know you guys had a bad breakup. I know things got rough. It's just, you know, where I come from, where most of these kids come from, getting slapped around by your man isn't that big of a thing. I'm just saying."

Colleen fought back the urge to turn on Bix. She wasn't ready to have this discussion, not with Bix, not here. Maybe not ever. She left it at, "It was a little more than getting slapped around."

"Yeah, I'm sure." She didn't sound convinced, but at least changed the topic. "But this is John we're talking about." She looked over at him helping one of the Green Fields girls onto the freight scale. "I do think he's cheating on me. For real this time."

Colleen watched as John laughed and applauded the girl's dance on the scale. "Has he ever cheated on you before?"

"No." Bix said it like a challenge. "I told you, I don't get cheated on. I won't stand for it. He knows that. I don't care about the drinking and the flirting. That's just John. But, you know, now . . . this." The threat of tears choked her voice. "I'm not getting any younger. And John has a lot of appetites, you know?"

"Oh Bix, no," Colleen said, hurrying to cut her off. The hangar full of kids was no place to have a discussion like this, especially with someone as volatile as Bix. Plus, Patrick made it sound as if John had been cheating on Bix for years. What could she say? *He isn't cheating on you because you're getting older. He's always cheated on you!*

Another eruption of laughter from the group at the freight scale and Bix shook her head.

"I'm telling you, it's this business. It's changed them. Both of them. When we started out, we just wanted to own our own business. Just be our own bosses. We thought we'd maybe have a couple of employees to give us some time off. Hell, one of the reasons we chose this business was so we could hire kids from Green Fields, give them some experience and job references."

"What changed?"

"Money." Bix said the word like it disgusted her. "It's like the more money we make, the more money they want. Like there was this threshold we crossed. Once Green Fields was up and running, once we got the fund-raising where we wanted it, it all became about the business. Making it bigger to make more money to make it bigger, and so on and so on."

"Well, isn't that how business works?" Colleen asked. "Grow or die?"

"Says the woman who's never had to work a day in her life." Bix held up her hand in surrender. "Sorry. Shitty again. Broken record. I apologize. It's just easier to be mad at you than to be mad at John."

"It's okay," Colleen said. It wasn't really. All anger unnerved Colleen and Bix's mercurial outbursts kept her feeling unsettled and raw. But apologies from Bix were rare and Colleen welcomed this one.

"I know it's okay," Bix said with a smile. "We're friends, right? I didn't know if we would be at first, but we are, aren't we?" She didn't wait for Colleen to agree. "That's cool. I'm glad. I don't know what I would do if I didn't have someone to talk to about this. And hell, for two women who have as little in common as we do, we share one big thing, don't we? We're both widows of the Macaroni Brothers campaign to greatness. You maybe even more than I am, since it looks like Pat's trying to work himself to death."

The rumble of machinery echoed through the hangar. Patrick was demonstrating how the enormous plane bay door operated while John led a group of girls on an inspection of the Cessna.

Bix pointed a long finger toward John. "I'm telling you, it's that god damned plane. That's what changed everything. Once Pat got his pilot's license and bought that damn plane, it was like they decided to be big shots. That's when they started fighting. That's when everything started turning to shit."

Mandy and Ginny began to call out for attention and, for the first time ever, Colleen felt relief at seeing the Green Fields bus pull around. If Bix blamed the troubles in her marriage on the purchase of the Cessna, the purchase Colleen had made possible, it wouldn't take long for Bix to drive that blame all the way back to Colleen.

Embracing the distraction, Colleen headed toward the bus to see the kids off. Patrick and John were all smiles, clapping kids on the shoulders, laughing and shouting along with them as they checked in with the counselors before boarding. Bix hurried to wrap up the left-over scones and lemon bars and hand them to the bus driver. Colleen ignored her dismissive wave. "You might as well take these. Someone might want them."

There was no point in getting irritated by it. The kids were gone. She had survived another field trip. There had been no fights, no calamities. Bix had remained relatively stable and had even called Colleen a friend. All they had to do was clean up and she could get away from the hangar.

Then she heard Patrick and John arguing.

Bix shot her a loaded look as she dragged a garbage can over to the food table. She and Colleen began dumping out the uneaten food as their husbands' voices grew louder.

"Because we made a deal, John," Patrick said. John's reply was muffled, although Colleen could clearly hear the word *bullshit* in there. The argument dropped in volume as the two men headed toward the office at the front of the hangar. Patrick seemed to be pursuing John, his face red as he spoke in low tones, while John just kept shaking his head.

"We need this," Patrick said, grabbing John's arm at last. "We can get another plane."

"We don't need it!" John shook off Patrick's grip. The last words Colleen could make out before the office door slammed shut were John's: "I'm telling you, man, I've got this under control."

The slam of the door rang through the hangar.

Bix pointed at Colleen with a greasy serving spoon. "I told you it is all about that god damn plane."

CHAPTER SIX

When it became clear Patrick and John had settled in for a long fight, both Colleen and Bix wanted to get out of the hangar. Colleen couldn't leave, however, since she'd ridden in with Patrick. Their post–field trip plan had made sense when they'd made it. He'd drop her off for a doctor's appointment, then run some errands nearby and swing back by for her. Easy. Except nothing was easy lately.

Bix came to her rescue, though, offering to drive her to her appointment while she ran some errands of her own. And Colleen was spared any further discussion of the damn plane's role in all their troubles, since Bix spent the entire drive on call after call, making appointments and returning calls from an agenda she apparently maintained purely by memory. She finished her final call as she slipped the SUV into a spot in front of the Gables Medical Center.

The sprawling, dark stone and glass building looked like a badly imagined mix of plantation home and upscale bank. As they headed for the smoked-glass doors, Colleen felt her usual dread rising.

A smiling young woman behind the registration desk squealed at Bix's arrival.

Bix grinned. "Hey, Tildie, how are you?"

Colleen stepped aside as the two women hugged and laughed, shouting out greetings to two other women who filed in from the back office. It seemed everyone knew Bix here. Colleen let them talk, signing in for her appointment. She was early, as always, and as always was in no hurry to get into the examination room. The only sense of urgency she felt hinged upon her desire to get out of the medical center as quickly as possible.

This was supposed to be her final post-surgery checkup. She had already decided that, regardless of Dr. Rimeroff's opinion, this would be her final visit to Gables ever.

Bix finished up her chatty reunion with the staff and followed Colleen down the hallway toward Rimeroff's office. They passed turn-offs to the surgery wing, post-op, dermatology, pediatrics, radiology, and cardiology. It went on and on. Gables Medical sprawled even more on the inside than its ugly exterior suggested.

"Remind me," Bix said, readjusting the purse that had been hugged loose by the women up front, "that I need to stop by the pharmacy when we're done here."

"We've got time," Colleen said, waving her into a quiet waiting room decorated in soft greens and browns. "I'm early and Rimeroff is always late. Why don't you go now?"

Bix flopped down in a chair and dropped her bag on the floor. "Because if I go now, I'll be stuck there for an hour talking with Sharon and Veena. I love those pharmacy girls but, god damn, they can talk the paint off the wall. If I go in with you, I can beg off and blame you for having to run."

Colleen laughed and settled in beside her. "I didn't realize you were in such demand around here."

"Well, I come in with the kids. I brought in that little boy from Frankfort whose appendix burst. And I have sat through three tonsil-lectomies since we started up Green Fields. And god only knows how many emergency room visits. You know how it is, kids wind up in hospitals."

"Aren't there nurses or counselors that can come?"

Bix shrugged. "Yeah, but I like to come. I remember how scary it was being in a hospital when I was a kid. Everything smells weird. All those weird noises. Every time my mom would leave, I'd freak the fuck out. I just figure I can spare a little time for them."

"I hate being here."

"Yeah, hospitals suck. At least this one is nice. Not like those big warehouse hospitals with people screaming and bleeding all over the place."

Colleen didn't bother to bring up that she herself had both screamed and bled within these walls. Instead, she changed the subject. "What medicine are you picking up?"

"I don't know. I'm going to see what they've got." At Colleen's surprised laugh, Bix shrugged again. "What? I always do that. Sharon always keeps some samples on hand for me. Dr. What's-His-Name from the kids' clinic gave me the go-ahead to get samples of Wellbutrin one time. Since then, Sharon and Veena both keep little goodie bags for me. I've gotten Xanax and allergy pills and Z-pak. You know, just to keep on hand."

"That can't be legal."

Bix laughed and shook her head. "You are precious, Colleen. It's perfectly legal and that's exactly what those samples are for. Those pharmaceutical reps bring that shit in by the carton hoping the doctors will pass it out and get people hooked on it. That's how the whole operation works."

"I think you're missing a step. You know—diagnosis, physician examination."

"For my money, I'll trust the nurses and the pharmacists before I trust a doctor."

"You mean for the money you're not paying?"

Bix nodded. "Exactly. Look, we have doctors coming in and out of Green Fields doing pro bono work. Gables gets their slice of government money for the aboveboard stuff. Way back when, Arlen Henderschott himself told us that the three of us could slip in here anytime we needed something. And he wasn't just talking about broken bones or heart attacks or anything. Someone will always help us out for little shit like sinus infections and the like."

Colleen refrained from commenting on Arlen Henderschott and his sweet deals, but her body language must have given her away. Bix clucked her tongue.

"Oh yeah, you're probably not a big fan of Arlen, are you? Less than impressed by the CEO of this medical empire?"

Colleen wouldn't look at her. "I'm sure he's very helpful to Green Fields."

Bix snickered. "And I'm sure that's probably your private school way of calling him a filthy fuck-stick. Am I right?" Colleen adjusted her purse in her lap, keeping her face neutral. Bix went on. "Yeah, that makes sense. Ex in-law and all that. Although technically, he's not an in-law, right? Or was he? Wait, how was he related to you?"

Colleen sighed, knowing she couldn't put Bix off the topic. "Arlen is married to Dilly Seaton, my ex-husband's older sister."

"Riiight," she said, then cocked her head. "So, I'm guessing that big divorce settlement probably pissed his wife off plenty, right? You took a bunch of old family money?" Colleen nodded. "So you and the Henderschotts in general are not such big fans of each other." Colleen kept nodding. "Then I've got to ask, why are we sitting here? I mean, are we here for . . . ?" She tipped her head forward, looking toward Colleen's stomach and back up at her face.

Colleen sighed. "Yes. It's my final checkup with the surgeon about the splenectomy."

"Splenectomy." Bix enunciated the word. "I see. And is there no other hospital in the city of Lexington that can perform splenectomies?

Is it a Gables exclusive? Because, I got to tell you, if my ex-husband beat me so bad I had to have my spleen removed, I probably wouldn't trust his brother-in-law to take it out. But that's just me."

"It was part of the divorce agreement." Colleen felt her cheeks warming just talking about that humiliating period of her life, when both sides argued monetary values for physical and psychological damages. "I agreed to complete all medical procedures related to . . ." She struggled to find words that wouldn't choke her. "I agreed to treat the immediate physical damages here at Gables, so there would be no question of future damages."

"'Future damages,'" Bix repeated. "That's a good one." When Colleen just shrugged, she went on. "So they want to control the spread of gossip and make sure you're not going to ride that gravy train forever." She shook her head. "Grabby fuckers. All that money and I bet they don't lose sight of a nickel. Well, whatever you got from the Seatons didn't seem to hurt old Arlen or his Gables franchise. Look at this place; it's huge. And he's got three more of these across the state and two in Indiana." She kept shaking her head. "And, of course, you got to keep all that money, so it wasn't a total loss."

"There are better ways to make money."

"And there are worse, trust me." Bix didn't give Colleen time to argue, even if she'd wanted to, which she didn't. "So this is your last checkup over this surgery? You don't have to come back after this?"

"You couldn't get me back into this building at gunpoint."

"Let me see your scar."

Colleen looked up at Bix to see if she was kidding. "Why?"

"Let me see it. Just lift up the edge of your shirt and let me see your scar. There's nobody in here. Nobody's going to see. Come on."

Feeling stupid both for obeying and for not thinking of a good reason to say no, Colleen lifted the hem of her blue sweater high enough to reveal the thin, straight scar along the center of her upper abdomen.

Bix leaned in closer to examine it. "Does it hurt?" Colleen started to lower the hem but Bix stopped her hand. "Is it sore?"

"No."

"Any cramping or abdominal pain?"

"What? No."

Bix pulled the sweater down to cover the scar. "Then I hereby pronounce you officially discharged. You have successfully survived your splenectomy and are free to go and have a cocktail with me."

"I can't, Bix. I have an appointment."

"You have a completely unnecessary appointment with a doctor who probably doesn't want to see you in a medical facility run by a man who would probably rather see you dead. At least his wife probably would, am I right?" Bix didn't bother to wait for a nod. "It's not like you had a heart transplant, Colleen. Trust me. My uncle had his spleen kicked out in a bar fight and his scar looked a hell of a lot worse than yours when they stopped his treatment because he was just using a medical card."

She really wasn't in the mood for one of Bix's family stories. "Bix, I have to—"

"You don't have to do shit, Colleen. You think this is about your surgery? Your health? Arlen Henderschott is just making his wife happy by making your life hell. He probably just wants to keep you jumping through hoops, make sure you never forget what happened to you. Fuck, you've got the money. Your scar is healed. You feel fine. All the rest is just passive-aggressive bullshit."

Colleen wanted to argue. People didn't just skip medical appointments. She had had surgery, and surgery required aftercare. Losing her spleen had been painful and had required certain lifestyle changes. She had to be careful now about catching colds or flus. She had to watch what she ate. This was serious.

On the other hand, she hated the way Dr. Rimeroff looked at her. She knew he consulted with Arlen Henderschott. She knew the surgeon was at least partly aware of the circumstances and arrangements around the surgery. He and Henderschott were old friends and country club buddies. Certainly Rimeroff had heard rumors about the end of her marriage. Colleen wondered why this had never occurred to her before.

She gathered her purse into her lap, keeping her eyes trained straight ahead, trying to organize her thoughts. Maybe Bix was right. Beside her, Bix sighed and settled back.

"I mean, I'll wait. If you want to see the doctor, I don't mind waiting with you."

She should see the doctor though, right? She had an appointment. She didn't know what to do, so she just sat there.

Bix unwrapped a piece of gum. "Does it bother you that Pat does jobs for Gables?"

"Yes."

"Whoa," Bix laughed. "No hesitation there. Have you told him it bothers you?"

"He just tells me it's business. That I wouldn't understand." Colleen didn't want to hear Bix's answer to that. She didn't want to talk about Patrick or their fight or Arlen Henderschott. "Screw this, Bix. You're right. Let's get out of here. Let's just go."

"Attagirl!" Bix slung her big purse up onto her shoulder. "You want to sneak out the back or do you want to flip off the nurses on the way out?"

"Your friends?" Colleen asked. "The ones out front?"

"Shit." Bix put her arm around Colleen. "They're just people I know. You're my friend. You want to get out of here, let's get the hell out of here and never darken the doorstep of Gables Medical again! Until, of course, I get a yeast infection or something and need free meds."

Colleen laughed and followed her toward the rear exit. "Until then."

From Gables, they headed off to run Bix's errands. They went from the county courthouse to the post office to an office at UK to a dentist office, as well as three office complexes Colleen couldn't identify. All the way, Bix took phone calls involving Macaroni Brothers business as well as Green Fields issues. At every stop, Bix reached into the back seat to pull out a file or an envelope or a package, always finding her target on the first try with no searching. She worked with a manic efficiency that mesmerized Colleen. It also kept her from worrying about the potential stupidity of skipping her doctor's appointment.

It was just after four when Bix climbed back into the SUV, unclipped her Bluetooth headset, and grinned.

"Done! Perfect timing, right? I got all that shit done in time for happy hour. You ready?"

Colleen had become so accustomed to Bix talking on the phone that it had taken a beat to realize Bix was speaking to her. It didn't matter. By the time she said yes, Bix had pulled out onto Winchester Road, headed for downtown.

. . . .

Bix pulled the SUV into a loading spot in front of One-Armed Harry's. Despite the rough-sounding name, the restaurant was an upscale gastropub with an excellent reputation, a world-class wine list, and the prices one would expect at such an establishment. Aside from a church, Colleen couldn't think of any place less likely to appeal to Bix.

"Are we going in?" she asked, since Bix had yet to shut off the engine. "I don't think we can park here."

Bix kept both hands on the wheel. "Have you ever eaten here?"

"Yeah, when it first opened. Heath took me here."

Bix looked at her as if she were studying her. "Did you like it?"

Had she liked it? It was impossible to remember anything from those days clearly. She remembered an expensive wine that stung the cuts on the inside of her lips. She recalled savory-looking tapas she couldn't smell because of her swollen nose that she had camouflaged with makeup. She remembered tall leather stools that came as a relief from the impossibly high heels Heath had made her wear.

"Well?" Bix asked again. "Did you like it?"

"I don't remember."

Bix kept her hands on the steering wheel. She chewed the edge of her lip and stared at the restaurant's façade.

"What are we doing, Bix?"

"This is where he goes. John. This is one of the places he's been drinking."

"That can't be cheap."

"It's not," Bix said. "Especially since he's buying drinks for someone else. I don't care how much liquor John can hold or how much they're charging for drinks, no one person can run up a bar tab that high."

"Are we going in?"

Bix's fingers tightened on the wheel. Her voice was a whisper. "I don't think I can. I thought I could. I thought I could march in there and that, if I saw him, I could get right up in his face. I thought if I saw him with whatever little whore he's running around with, I could grab her by the hair and drag her out to the curb and beat the shit out of her." Tears shimmered on her lashes and her voice broke. "But I don't think I can do that. What if he just laughs at me, Colleen? What if he doesn't even care?"

Colleen reached out to loosen Bix's fingers from the wheel. "Talk to me. What is going on?" She hated the position she found herself in. Thanks to Patrick, she knew Bix was probably right in her suspicions, but she couldn't bear to worsen her friend's misery. On the other hand, she felt terrible prolonging what seemed to be inevitable. "Why are you all of a sudden convinced that John's drinking has turned to cheating?"

Bix let out a loud sigh and turned off the vehicle. From her purse, she pulled out a cell phone Colleen had never seen her use before. She thumbed the screen to life and held it up for Colleen to see.

"What is it?" She squinted, trying to make sense of the blurry photo. "I can't tell what that . . . oh. Oh."

"Yeah," Bix said, thumbing through the phone some more. "And just in case you hadn't been able to make out that picture, here's one of the texts that came along with it." She held the phone up for Colleen to read the message.

$$$ = *big titties*

"Subtle."

"Yeah," Bix snorted. "Even I think it's tacky, so you know that's something. That's not even the best one. Here's a nice one. *Got sweet pussy—let's deal.* And this one's nice." She held up a picture of a red handprint on what looked like a smooth, brown thigh. Colleen looked away.

"Where did you get these pictures? Is that John's phone?"

"Sort of." Bix put the phone on the dashboard.

"Sort of?"

She nodded. "Sort of. John and Pat wanted new phones a few months ago when they decided to become big shots. Of course they expected me to set them all up, so I did. And when I did, I made sure to clone John's phone."

"Clone it?" Colleen asked. "I thought that was just a thing TV cops did."

"No, it's a real thing. Not that hard, either, especially when you have all the passwords and SIM cards. It took me, like, ten minutes online to figure out how to do it. I told you. I will not be cheated on."

They both looked at the silent phone on the dashboard, knowing it held evidence to the contrary.

"Do you know who he's talking to?"

Bix shook her head.

"How long has it been going on?"

"A few weeks. At first, when I set this up, I thought I'd been stupid. I thought I'd overreacted." She smiled a sad smile at Colleen. "Can

64

you imagine me worrying about overreacting? But there was nothing happening. I found out John golfs a lot more than he admits to and he really does almost no work anymore, but that's no big thing. Then these started coming in. And the fights started getting worse between him and Pat."

Tears rolled back in. "And now I'm afraid I'm going to lose him, Colleen. I'm going to lose everything."

A selfish anxiety twisted in Colleen's gut. If Bix and John broke up, that would badly disrupt the business, which would make her already overworked and tense husband frantic. She felt bad for Bix, truly she did, but Colleen couldn't hide from the dread she felt at the thought of losing the small acre of peace she had carved out with Patrick.

She swallowed all that down, ordered herself to do the right thing by her friend. "What can I do to help?"

Bix squeezed her hand. "You're the best, Colleen. I knew I could count on you." She nodded toward the pub's door. "Will you go in and see if John's there? Tell me if he's with anyone? He got a text this morning saying four o'clock."

"What do you want me to do if he's here?"

"Get a picture of her. See if you can overhear her name."

"He'll see me!"

"No he won't," Bix said. "Nobody is going to notice you if they're sitting next to a hot set of tits. I mean, you know what I mean. Just see what you can see."

Colleen couldn't see anything for it but to agree and slipped out of the SUV. This was a stupid plan. Despite Bix's insulting assurance, Colleen knew she would not be invisible in One-Armed Harry's. For one thing, it was early. She doubted there would be a crowd. For another, this wasn't the kind of place where women wore riding boots and sweater sets. Still, she promised Bix she'd do her best.

Inside the dark pub, the walls were lined with copper plates and sconces that bounced dim light around with a warm glow. As she expected, the place was nearly empty. A couple of young women laughed at one end of the bar and two rumpled businessmen watched television over martinis.

Colleen sidled up to one of the tall leather stools she had remembered correctly and heard, from a booth to her right, a familiar easy laugh. A laugh she would know anywhere.

John.

She turned slowly, not wanting to catch his attention, and saw him kicked back in a booth, clinking glasses with someone she would also know anywhere.

Heath Seaton.

. . . .

"Start the car."

Colleen slammed the door hard. Her hands shook as she tried to buckle her seat belt.

"Was he there? Did you see him?"

"Start the car!"

Bix jumped when Colleen yelled, hurrying to start the SUV and pulling out into traffic. "What the fuck, Colleen? What happened? Did you see him?"

"Just drive." She breathed in hard through her nose, trying to calm herself. Trying to wrap her head around what she had just seen.

"Colleen, if you don't tell me what the fuck you saw, I swear to god I'm going to pull this car over and beat the shit out of you."

"Heath Seaton. John was sitting with Heath Seaton."

"Were there girls?" When Colleen spun on her, Bix held her hands up in confusion. "What? I don't give a shit what guys he's drinking with. I want to know who's sending him tit pics. Fuck, Colleen, this isn't about you, okay? It's about me. It's about my marriage, not your getting all twisted because you saw your ex."

Colleen struggled to calm down. She had to explain this to Bix. She had to make the other woman understand how serious this was.

"Bix," she said, willing her voice steady, "Heath Seaton is a very bad person. I know you think I don't know what bad is, but trust me: I do. Heath does *very* bad things, and does them for no other reason than that he can. If John is drinking with him, if John is making any kind of deals with him, you have a lot more to worry about than just an affair."

Bix bit her lip as she sped along the city street. "You think they're running whores."

"I have no idea what that even means, but if it's bad, if it's illegal and incredibly degrading and dangerous to any woman it touches, then yes. That is definitely a possibility."

"What do you think we should do?"

Colleen shut her eyes. What she wanted to do was go home, climb into a hot shower, and scrub off even this distant encounter with her ex-husband. That wouldn't solve the problem at hand, however.

"What do the texts say?" Colleen asked. "All of them? Do they mention anything specific about girls or drugs or anything?"

"Well, there's all kinds of mentions of making deals for pussy, so yeah. That's pretty specific. And there's a list of names. Girls' names."

"That John had?"

"No," Bix said. "That whoever it was sent to John. There was no name saying who it was, just a cell number. You think he's dealing with Heath?"

"They looked awfully cozy. And Heath doesn't get cozy with anyone he can't use."

Bix kept chewing on that lip. "What do you think I should do?"

Colleen forced her shoulders to relax. "I think you should find out who those girls are on that list."

"You could do that, right?" All of a sudden, Bix sounded young. "You have that attorney, don't you? The one who got you all that money from your divorce. You said she found out all sorts of shit about Heath. You think she could find out who these girls are?"

Colleen dropped her head back against the seat, her initial terror fading as the distance from Heath grew. "I don't know, Bix. This is not what she does. I don't want to ask her for this."

"Please, Colleen." Tears shone in Bix's eyes. "John is all I have. And he's Patrick's best friend. If John's doing something stupid, please help me find out what it is."

Colleen nodded, thinking less about Bix and more about that little acre of peace she loved so much.

CHAPTER SEVEN

Friday, October 2

Alyssa Rovito gripped the back of the chair and stared down at Colleen.

"Don't stand up. I am not sitting down. I am not ordering lunch. I'm not even going to say hello until you can make me a promise. Will you make this promise? Will you?"

Colleen's mouth went dry. She didn't know what Alyssa was talking about, what she could possibly want sworn, why she looked so angry to see her. She nodded.

Alyssa went on, traces of her New Jersey accent coming through her serious tone. "Swear to me on all that you hold holy that you are not here to corral me onto the reunion committee. Swear it!" She waited for Colleen to catch on.

"Oh. No. No!" Relief blew out on a laugh as Alyssa dropped the stern act and came around to hug Colleen. Alyssa's heels put her over six feet. Her copper-colored dress looked expensive and she wore her blond hair pinned up with messy elegance. Alyssa Rovito dressed to intimidate. She was smart, cunning, and ruthless. In other words, she was the perfect divorce attorney. She also happened to have been Colleen's roommate for three years in boarding school.

"You're getting hammered by their emails, too, aren't you?" Alyssa asked, taking her seat. "Three a day. Minimum. Every day. My god, I didn't get this much communication from them when I volunteered for the endowment fund."

"I am getting the emails. Every day. I haven't even decided if I'm going yet."

Alyssa looked at her over the menu. "Oh you have to go. It's our twentieth. We both look fantastic, so we have to go. If you don't go, people will think you got fat."

Colleen cackled. Alyssa had always been able to make her laugh, even during the darkest days of the divorce. "Okay, I'll go if you go, but I'm not on the committee to run the thing."

"Absolutely not. I give to the endowment fund. I don't stuff gift bags."

The waiter arrived and took their order. Alyssa waited until he delivered their iced tea before she crossed her hands on the table and leaned forward.

"By the way, before we get started, I still haven't forgiven you for standing me up for the Catholic Daughters luncheon. Did you know what the charity was last month?" Colleen shook her head. "The Skin Bank. Did you know there was an organization called the Skin Bank? Skin donations? Yeah." They grimaced in unison. "Yeah. They really should have rethought serving lasagna for that."

Colleen had to laugh. "Glad I missed it."

"You are," Alyssa said seriously. "Trust me. So if you're not here for St. Ag's and you're not here to make amends for my lasagna nightmares, what's up? Everything okay? Am I wearing my girlfriend hat or my attorney hat?"

"Both, maybe? Neither, sort of?"

"Oh that clears it up. Is it about Patrick?"

"No. Not exactly. I mean, not directly." Alyssa arched a perfectly shaped brow and Colleen hurried to put that thought to rest. "No, no. I'm not looking into divorce."

She nodded. "I don't judge."

"I know."

Alyssa had been less than enthusiastic about Colleen's marriage to Patrick so soon after the divorce. She'd assured Colleen that it wasn't a dislike of Patrick, but more a wariness of her vulnerability after the trauma and brutality of her marriage to Heath. But Colleen had been so damaged afterwards, physically and emotionally. Patrick was so calm, so solid and practical and decent in ways Heath could only imagine. Marrying Patrick had helped heal her, so Alyssa had put her concerns to the side and agreed to be Colleen's matron of honor at the courthouse ceremony.

She had drafted the prenup as her wedding gift.

"Is it business-related?" Alyssa asked, fishing. "How is business these days?"

"Good, I suppose. They're busy. They're trying to grow. Get bigger freight jobs, steadier clients. They finished their move to the new hangar. It's enormous. I feel like I have to leave a trail of bread crumbs every time I go inside. Patrick has been flying a lot."

"It's nice to know your money is going to good use."

"He paid me back, Alyssa. Three weeks early, as a matter of fact."

"That's impressive. It was a lot of money." Alyssa knew just how much, because she wrote up the debt agreement at Patrick's insistence, so there would be no question about his intentions to pay it back.

"Yes, it was." Colleen picked a lemon seed out of her tea and flicked it across the table. "So yeah, business is good."

"Good." She softened her tone at Colleen's glare. "No really. That's good. That's very good, and I'm glad to hear that Patrick takes your money seriously. That he takes the business seriously. I am glad. You deserve a responsible man. I like Patrick."

"He's a good man."

"I know he is. And I know he's come up from some hard circumstances and that's probably why he takes borrowing money so seriously and I respect that. He's not an entitled douche bag like Heath Seaton." They toasted each other with their iced tea. "Which makes me wonder why he chooses to do business with the people he does. I've told you this before and, as your attorney, I will tell you this again for free." She held up her hand to hold the thought as the waiter set down their sandwiches. She checked to make sure nobody was within earshot.

"I don't understand why the Macaroni Brothers are in business with Arlen Henderschott."

Colleen sighed. Alyssa had brought this up many times before, more times even than Colleen had brought it up with Patrick. "I've told you, it's just business."

"It's never just business with Arlen Henderschott and you know it. He's a piece of shit."

"I know."

"He practically runs a pill mill and he's a hack. He's bought himself out of countless sexual harassment charges and malpractice suits. That chain of medical centers he's part of has been investigated for tax evasion so many times the IRS probably has a field office at their corporate headquarters."

"I know, Alyssa, but Patrick and John are just doing freight jobs for them, not running the operating room. Gables is a very lucrative client. They can't afford to turn down the business."

Alyssa pointed at Colleen with a potato chip. "Doesn't that make you wonder? Why does an outfit like Gables Medical, the epitome of cronyism and old boy network, hire a company like Macaroni Brothers? Did you ever ask yourself that?"

Colleen fiddled with her sandwich. She had never wanted to put it into words, but now that Alyssa had, the question seemed obvious.

"No offense to the Macaroni Brothers or your husband, but there are a dozen companies who can do what they do and they're probably owned by other old white men like Arlen Henderschott. So why give the work to Patrick? It's not like Henderschott to want to spread the wealth around. He's certainly not known for hobnobbing with the masses."

"I know."

Colleen felt pressured to defend Patrick but Alyssa had one more bullet in her gun.

"And on top of all of that, Arlen Henderschott is married to your former sister-in-law, the woman who tried to convince the police to press battery charges against *you* when her little brother kicked your spleen out."

"I know!" Colleen checked herself and lowered her voice. "Do you think I don't know that? Do you think I've forgotten any of that?"

"I don't know, Colleen. Have you? Because you're married to a man who is doing business with these people."

"He's doing business with Gables Medical."

Alyssa grabbed her hand. "He's doing business with the Henderschotts. You can't separate the man from the business. And that reptile wife of his." She put Colleen's hand down. "If you took all of Heath Seaton's malice and perversion and gave it ambition and a brain, you would get Dilly Seaton Henderschott. Christ, they even look alike."

"I know."

She did. She knew all too well what Dilly Seaton Henderschott was capable of because she'd been on the losing end of Dilly's little brother's mental aberrations. She had the scars to prove it.

Colleen looked down at the club sandwich she'd been looking forward to. Her appetite had fled. But judging by the look on Alyssa's face, the conversation wasn't over.

"Have you told Patrick everything?"

With that, Colleen figured she wouldn't be wanting dinner tonight, either.

"Yes."

"Everything?" Alyssa leaned forward. "All of it? Not just the beatings. All of it."

Humiliation bloomed over Colleen's face and tears rose in her eyes. "I told him enough."

Alyssa sighed. "And he's still doing business with them."

Colleen dropped her head into her hands. "What do you want me to say? They're a small business. It's a crap economy. The medical center isn't their only client and they're not in bed with the Gables chain. Patrick flies some short hops for the center—delivering samples or records, sometimes transporting a doctor from one facility to another. Each of the Gables facilities has a pilot like Patrick. It pays the bills. Plus, the medical center provides services for the kids at Green Fields."

"Oh that sounds good," Alyssa said. "Putting Arlen Henderschott around children. What could go wrong?"

"Trust me. Arlen Henderschott has never stepped foot in Green Fields. He's probably afraid poverty is contagious."

"Probably," Alyssa said. "Or maybe he's afraid one of the kids will slip and fall in that trail of slime he leaves behind him and sue him."

Alyssa pushed her untouched sandwich to the side. It seemed the conversation had killed both of their appetites.

"Okay, I will drop the Arlen Henderschott lynching for the moment, knowing that it will come back into play. If you're ever going to need a lawyer, it's going to involve the Gables Medical Center. But until then, what did you want to ask me about?"

Colleen reached for her purse. She hadn't anticipated Alyssa's tangent. It felt beyond awkward to bring up anything involving Heath now, even indirectly, but there was nothing for it but to pull out the list of names Bix had written down. As Alyssa read them to herself, Colleen said, "I need to see who these people are, why they would be on a list together. I'm not sure exactly what I'm looking for. Just give them to your guy who does your investigating and see if he can find any kind of connection between them. If any kind of bells go off."

Alyssa hummed as she stared at the list. "Adkins, Bias, Kilgore. These are pretty common names. I sat in on a deposition in Lawrence County over the summer. There were twenty-five people in the room; fifteen of them were named Adkins. Is there anything particular I'm looking for? Can you give me some kind of direction? Where did you get this list?"

Colleen didn't want to answer that, knowing the conversation was getting ready to take another hard turn. "Bix Mulroney found it on her husband's phone."

Alyssa fell back into her chair and groaned toward the ceiling.

"She thinks John is cheating on her."

Groan.

"And she thinks these might be hookers or girls they're doing drugs with."

"What do you mean 'they'? Girls John and who else is doing drugs with?"

"John has been spending time with Heath. Running around with him."

Alyssa dragged herself forward and held the note up between them.

"You're killing me, Colleen. Slowly and surely, you are killing me."

"I know this isn't your thing and you don't like to get involved in domestic stuff like this and I wouldn't ask except that John is Patrick's partner and his best friend. If John is getting mixed up in something with Heath—"

"Wait, wait. Stop." She waved the note at Colleen, glaring at her with a look that in high school would have been accompanied by a slap upside the head. "Bix Mulroney wants you to ask me to look up these names. She wants me to work for her through you."

"I said I would ask—"

"First of all, that takes a lot of nerve. If she wants to hire me, she can ask me herself and pay her own fees. I'm not her attorney or her friend. Secondly, and more importantly, why is Bix Mulroney worried about these names? Are you telling me that Bix Mulroney"—she spat out the name like a bug she'd swallowed—"is afraid that John is sleeping with cheap whores? Why would he be? He married one."

"Don't say that."

"You know, I don't consider myself a snob. I have friends from all walks of life." Alyssa's waving hands nearly knocked over her tea. "I don't think money equals class and I don't believe in discounting people by where they came from. And I don't use this phrase lightly. But in this case, it is perfectly accurate. Bix Mulroney is trash. And I can't believe you are spending time with her. Much less doing favors for her."

Colleen took a deep breath and kept quiet, giving Alyssa time to calm down. It took a while. Alyssa held the list up again. "We always said we would do anything for each other, but this might be too much to ask."

"I'm not asking for Bix. I don't care what goes on in their marriage. I know Bix can be a handful but she's—"

"She's a disaster, Colleen." Alyssa talked over her. "She's a nightmare. I sat at the same table with her at the Rotary meeting where John Mulroney was giving a presentation about Green Fields. Bix got so drunk—at a Rotary luncheon, mind you—that she slapped a piece of ham on Rabbi Wucher's sandwich and dared him to eat it to see if Yahweh would strike him dead."

"Oh my god. I hadn't heard that."

"Really? I'm surprised, because everyone was talking about it. Everyone. Everywhere. She is a train wreck."

Colleen closed her eyes. "I know it's hard to believe, but she actually has a good side. She's really good with the kids at Green Fields and—"

"So what? Golden retrievers are good with kids, too. It doesn't mean I would invite one to sit at a table with adults."

"What do you want me to say, Alyssa?" Hunger and aggravation sharpened her tone. "She's married to my husband's best friend and business partner. Patrick would literally do anything for John, anything, no questions asked. They are lifelong best friends and as long as I'm married to Patrick and Bix is married to John, we have to be friends, too. And you know what? There's a lot to like about Bix. You might actually like her if—"

"I am never going to like Bix Mulroney."

Colleen threw her napkin down. "Who *do* you like, Alyssa? Anyone?"

There was that stare again.

"I like you, Colleen. I miss you. When I moved down here after my divorce, I thought we'd see each other more. We have been friends for twenty years and now I never see you. What happened to you, Colleen?"

Colleen stared at the table. "You of all people should know that."

"I don't mean the stuff with Heath. I know that was horrible but I also know you. Or at least I knew you." She took Colleen's hand again. "What happened to Mad Dog Dooley?"

Now it was Colleen's turn to groan at the ceiling.

"My mom still has that picture of you framed in her living room. You know the one I'm talking about." Alyssa grinned. "You were pitching to that fat girl from Trinity who kept running her mouth. You drilled her right in the ass and she knew it."

"Stop," Colleen said, trying not to laugh.

"You never threw a wild pitch and she knew you hit her on purpose. Do you remember? She came roaring out at you, twice your size and easily a hundred pounds heavier, and you beat her ass."

Colleen laughed and Alyssa went on.

"My mom got the picture of the umpire pulling you off, you climbing over him, nothing but fists and teeth and blood. My parents laughed and laughed at that. They loved that you were my roommate."

Alyssa squeezed her fingers. "Of course, they didn't know how outrageous you were. Nobody did. Everyone thought you were such a goody two-shoes."

"I was a goody-two-shoes!"

"Are you kidding me? You taught me how to sneak out of Baker Hall and climb up onto the roof. And don't think I've forgotten your famous art exhibit."

"Oh my god," Colleen laughed and covered her eyes with her free hand.

"Yeah, remember that? Junior year?" She could barely speak through her grin. "Your big calligraphy project. What was the quote? Such high-flown, flowery shit." She closed her eyes and tried working it out. "'For unless Conscience knows Truth, history is . . .' What? Something *s*."

"'Static,'" Colleen supplied.

"Right, 'history is static.' I was going to say *silent*. So it's 'For unless Conscience knows Truth, history is static. See Hope . . .'" Alyssa slapped the table with her palm. "Damn it! Give it to me."

Colleen sighed. "'For unless Conscience knows Truth, history is static. See Hope itself tremble.'"

"Yes!" Again Alyssa punished the tabletop, not caring that people were staring. "God, so incredibly deep."

Colleen cackled loudly and then covered her mouth but Alyssa wasn't finished.

"That picture was still hanging in Millory Hall at the last reunion. I'll bet it still is. Everybody was so impressed with your depth and wisdom. Who'd think to see what happened when you put the first letters of each word in order."

"Fuck this shit."

"Fuck this shit." Alyssa gasped the words out around her laugh. "You wrote *fuck this shit* in coded calligraphy and got the headmistress of St. Agatha's to hang it in the entrance hall. You did that, Colleen. You. Mad Dog Dooley. You were hilarious. You were outrageous."

Colleen kept her eyes behind her hand.

"That's who I like, Coll. Mad Dog Dooley. I miss her. I want my friend back."

"That was a long time ago. A lot has happened."

"I know. But I also know that she's still in there." Colleen wiped at her tears to look at her old friend whose eyes were also damp. "Mad Dog Dooley is still in there. She might be scared. I know she took a real beating, but I also know how tough she is."

Colleen looked away. "Maybe she ran off when they took out my spleen."

"Nah," Alyssa whispered. "She wouldn't leave you. And neither will I." She picked up the list. "I'll see what I can find about these names."

CHAPTER EIGHT

Saturday, October 3

The opening weekend of Keeneland.

Colleen hadn't been this excited for a Saturday in months. No, all year. Since last October. She'd missed the April season this year, claiming she was too happy, still in her honeymoon phase with Patrick. It was partially true but the bigger part of the truth was that she hadn't been ready to face the familiar crowds at the racetrack. Despite the closure of the divorce settlement and her recovery from the worst of her physical wounds, Colleen still hadn't been ready to take the chance of running into Heath Seaton at the one place they'd both loved.

Her lunch with Alyssa had loosened something up inside Colleen. She knew she was a far cry from the wild-spirited teenager her old roommate reminisced about, but just the memory of that courage warmed up corners of her mind that had long gone cold.

She wasn't missing another season.

Plus, seeing how Patrick looked in his lightweight blue suit? Even if she couldn't avoid bumping into Heath today, maybe there would be a payoff in showing him how well she had replaced him.

Colleen's parents had been members of the Keeneland Club her entire life and they'd kept that membership up despite retiring to Pawleys Island several years ago. Membership was strictly limited. People waited decades to make the list. The only way to get a space in the club was for a standing member to pass away without bequeathing the membership to an heir. Alyssa had talked about going after Heath's membership during the divorce, hitting him in the soul as well as the pocketbook, but like Colleen, Heath's admittance came under the family name and there was no universe in which the Seatons would be removed from Keeneland.

Just because Keeneland kept the membership limited didn't mean it wouldn't be crowded. Unlike other racetracks around the country, Keeneland had only two short seasons—April and October. Their money came from the breeding and sales of thoroughbreds. This meant that when the track opened, everyone attended. Members of the Keeneland Club could invite guests and the line for will-call tickets outside the Clubhouse was never short.

Colleen didn't mind the crowds. She didn't feel the social pressure. Keeneland was about the only place on earth Colleen didn't feel self-conscious. To her, it had always been a magical place, a place her parents would take her and her sisters, all of them in skirts and sweaters, Daddy in one of his funny plaid blazers. The girls were allowed to run free on the lawn and Colleen had never tired of seeing the massive horses thundering along the rail.

Tradition meant everything at Keeneland. From the bugle player to the savory burgoo stew to the unbreakable dress code, Keeneland never changed and Colleen loved it.

It always seemed to Colleen that the men bore the heavier burden under the Clubhouse dress code—jackets had to be worn at all times, while women were simply expected to dress appropriately. Maybe the standards for women were never expressed in writing because of the unspoken tradition of race season—the fashion display put on by women of a certain age, what Colleen's sisters used to call the Husband Lure. The Dooley girls used to laugh at these young women, many of whom had worked hard to wrangle a pass into the Clubhouse, who preened and pranced in haute couture. The Dooley girls had never dressed like that.

Keeneland was about horses and the Dooley girls always wore boots.

Today was no exception. Slim wool pants, high riding boots, a blue twin set, and a heavy plaid scarf and Colleen felt as at home strolling through the limestone walkways of Keeneland as she felt in her own living room. All around, men in blazers and club ties escorted women in dresses and heels. Air kisses were thrown and fashions admired. Patrick held her elbow as they got the invisible ink hand stamp that allowed them to come and go from the Clubhouse if they wished.

Patrick had only hinted at his excitement at having access to the Clubhouse. John and Bix had cracked jokes about getting nosebleeds from the rarefied air of the private space, which led Colleen to believe that they, too, were excited about being allowed in. Nothing said Lexington like thoroughbred racing and bourbon, and no place did them better than the Keeneland Clubhouse.

They all had their reasons to want to be here. Patrick wanted to network. John wanted shorter drink lines. Bix kept talking about seeing the magnificent horses up close.

But Colleen knew just where she wanted to be. On the patio outside the glass doors, underneath the brilliant October sun, with nothing between her and the perfectly groomed dirt track except bluegrass. As the day went on, people would move from the betting booths inside to the rail of the track, back and forth all day long, and that was just fine with her. Unlike many of the folks in heels, she could easily cut across the grass when she wanted to stand railside. Boots didn't sink into the turf like stilettos and would suffer no damage should the ground be muddy.

She and Patrick were early at her insistence. Colleen left guest passes for John and Bix at will-call. The races didn't start until one but Colleen didn't want to waste a second of race season. Patrick took the seat opposite her at the little table.

"Now that is a smile I love to see," he said, grinning at her. "You love it here."

"I do."

"I'm glad we came. I was sorry we didn't make it in April."

She shrugged. "We made it now. October is the best season, anyway. Better weather to eat burgoo." She laughed at his grimace. "Don't tell me you don't eat burgoo!"

"Well," he shook his head, "I don't know what they put in the burgoo at Keeneland, but where I grew up, *burgoo* was code for *roadkill stew*. And I make it a policy never to eat anything that might contain possum."

Colleen laughed. "How about this? We get the burgoo and if you so much as suspect there's possum meat in it, I'll eat yours, too."

"Sounds like a clever plan for you to eat all the burgoo. Am I being played?"

"Definitely."

The breeze picked up, blowing puffy white clouds around overhead, ruffling Patrick's hair and letting the sun play across his smiling face. With the background chatter of race statistics over the loudspeaker and the oddly fragrant aroma of mud, grass, and horse manure, Colleen thought she might be experiencing one utterly perfect moment.

So perfect that even the arrival of Arlen and Dilly Seaton Henderschott couldn't ruin it.

Dampen, but not ruin.

She saw Arlen first, his weirdly smooth face, skin like melted wax poured over a skull, oversized false teeth that should have been whiter pushing out his thin, wet lips. She always expected him to be taller, but the crowd made it obvious he barely cleared five feet seven. At least he had stopped dyeing his hair coal black. Now his thick hair had a greasy gray sheen, comb marks evident from forehead to the back of his skull. He took his time coming through the crowd at the patio doors, stopping to smile and shake hands with half a dozen people gathered there.

Those people parted to make way for the one Colleen knew came right behind him—Dilly Seaton Henderschott. Taller than her husband and at least a dozen years younger, Dilly carried herself like an empress, her thin chin high enough to pull her already taut skin even tighter. The blond hair that was a Seaton trademark didn't move, sprayed into submission to hold a rigid, chin-length bob that swung out beneath her jaw in points sharp enough to take an eye out.

Nobody could call Dilly unattractive, at least not in theory. Her skin shone with golden health. She moved her razor-slim figure with easy grace. She even smiled. In theory. Although to Colleen it looked a lot more like baring her teeth. Still, the crowd that moved aside to let her through stood close waiting to greet her, allowing her thin hands to clutch theirs, leaning in to receive the greetings she would deliver in her low, throaty tone.

But it was her eyes that most unnerved Colleen. Pale blue eyes, heavy-lidded, that moved slowly over a room, missing nothing. Eyes that could focus on you like a rifle sight and make you believe you deserved to be trapped in the crosshair. Alyssa described them as "dead eyes" but Colleen didn't find that description wholly accurate. *Killer eyes* might be more on target. Predatory, like the eyes of a snake in a world full of mice.

Heath had those eyes. Colleen had been his mouse for years.

Not today. Patrick leaned back in his chair, breaking her line of sight to the Henderschotts, his soft brown eyes squinting to read the race lineup on the marquee. "Are we betting?" he asked, oblivious to her distress. Good. Her panic didn't show. It didn't control her anymore. She was going to keep it that way.

"We should bet something," she said, flipping open the program. "It makes the races more fun. Who do you like? What do you want to bet?"

He made a funny face and leaned across the table. "Would you think less of me as a man if I told you I have no idea how to bet? I've never bet on a race before."

"What?" Colleen laughed. "I thought you and John used to bet all the time."

"Nope, just John. He loves to gamble. I would just tag along." He shrugged at her surprise. "How about this? You pick who to bet on and I'll get us a drink. And when I come back, you tell me what to do so that I don't look like an idiot and I'll go place our bet."

If he hadn't already seemed perfect enough, he stopped before he turned from the table, leaned down, and gave her a kiss. "Pick a winner," he whispered.

"I already did."

She got another kiss for that.

As she watched him cut through the crowd toward the outside bar, she almost asked herself what she had done to deserve a man like Patrick McElroy, a man who didn't gamble, who didn't have to pretend to know everything, a man who respected her opinion and openly admired her. She almost asked herself what she had done and then she remembered—she had survived a man who was Patrick's opposite in every way—a vain, spoiled, sadistic child.

"Fuck you, Heath Seaton," Colleen whispered to herself. She'd been saying those words for over a year, trying to make herself believe them. Today they rolled off her lips with authority.

God, she loved Keeneland.

Bix and John arrived after the second race and at the end of Colleen's first glass of white wine. Bix took Patrick's seat and sent John off to get them a round of drinks.

Patrick brought Colleen a cup of burgoo with an extra pile of crackers. "Just in case you decide to try to keep up with Bix on the cocktails," he said with a wink.

Bix sniffed the brown stew. "What is that?"

"Burgoo," Colleen said, stirring up a spoonful of beef and corn. Bix grimaced. "What kind of Kentucky girl are you that you don't know burgoo?"

"The kind that doesn't eat possum."

Colleen laughed, not bothering to correct her. John dropped off their drinks—another white wine for her, a beer for Bix—and then he and Patrick headed into the crowd. Bix took a sip and then scowled at her cup.

"This fancy-ass Clubhouse and we're drinking out of plastic cups?"

"Yes we are," Colleen said, the wine loosening her tongue. She waved her cup toward the rail. "Those are million-dollar animals running past us. They're highbred and high-strung. Nobody is going to take a chance on some idiot shattering a glass and spooking one of them. So plastic it is."

"Here's to plastic." A tap of the cups and they both drank. Bix lowered her drink and leaned in toward Colleen. "And speaking of plastic, how many sets of fake boobs do you suppose we are looking at right now? It's like a Barbie convention."

Colleen laughed and scooted her chair closer to Bix. Patrick had wandered off to make small talk; John had gone inside, probably to place his bets. The wine and the sunshine had combined to relax Colleen until the thought of gossip with Bix sounded just fine. She pointed out the Husband Lures and the men they were trying to catch. They commented on bad suits and worse face-lifts, silly catty gossip that made them both laugh.

Before the fourth race, Bix scanned the crowd to pick someone new to discuss and then she elbowed Colleen hard. "There. Three o'clock."

Colleen looked to her left, over Bix's shoulder. "Your other three o'clock, genius," Bix snorted, nodding over Colleen's right shoulder.

Colleen scanned the crowd for whatever particular vision had captured Bix's attention. At first she thought it was a very drunk-looking skinny girl in thigh-high boots and a tacky mink shrug. Then she saw that girl stumble and reach out to steady herself on the man beside her.

Heath Seaton.

Bix muttered, "I guess horse manure isn't the only shit that's lying around out here."

Colleen had drunk enough wine not to drop into that terrified paralysis she knew so well. Her heart only kicked at her ribs rather than trying to blast through them, and for the first time in a long time, Colleen thought she might survive an encounter with her ex-husband. The odds improved if this encounter remained visual-only, but Colleen considered this a win.

"Fuck him." Colleen toasted Bix, who barked out a laugh.

"Man, you even make that word sound classy. Must be all that private school."

"Indeed."

After the sixth race, Colleen decided to head to the patio bar to get another round. She had two good reasons for this. One, the more she drank, the better the wine tasted and the funnier Bix became, and two, she wanted to be sure she could still walk straight. That burgoo wouldn't hold her forever. She made her way through the crowd on relatively steady feet, thankful for the low-heeled riding boots. Two loose lines made their way to a pair of frazzled yet smiling bartenders.

In front of her, three young women leaned against each other, laughing at their boyfriends who stood near the rail, waving cigars. Their drink order sounded complicated and lengthy. Colleen had turned half away from the bar, knowing she had a wait, when she saw that in the other line, just over her right shoulder, stood Heath and his very skinny, now even drunker-looking girlfriend.

He was smiling at Colleen, had obviously been waiting for her to turn around. She felt that familiar coldness run through her body. His pale blue eyes didn't blink. His pink lips drew back to reveal those small, even, white teeth that were so much more dangerous than they appeared. Whatever booze or pills he had chosen for the day had turned his peaches-and-cream complexion a mottled berry color, but to the people who didn't know him the way Colleen did, Heath Seaton looked like the poster boy for good, clean, aristocratic breeding.

"Fuck you," she whispered, trying not to move her mouth, trying not to give him the satisfaction, trying not to lose the conviction those words had held earlier. She wasn't scared of Heath anymore. Well, that's what she planned on believing, so, against every instinct in her body, she turned back toward the bar, turned her back on the face of her nightmares.

She hoped it looked dismissive.

The drunk girls finally wrangled their load of plastic cups, spilling far too much to have made the wait worthwhile. Colleen gave them room to step away and had just given her order to the bartender when she could sense Heath behind her. Close to her. The fuzz of the skinny girl's mink shrug broke the edges of her peripheral vision and Colleen concentrated on the money in her hands, on the bar activity before her, on the race announcements in the air.

Anything but the certainty that, at any second, Heath would yank her by the hair, drag her to the ground, snarling and biting. She could feel her scalp crawling with dread.

Instead, she heard him singing.

No words, just a three-note scale, descending.

Bum bum bum.

Then an octave lower.

Bum bum bum.

Not much of a tune, but something in it felt familiar to Colleen. He repeated the sequence again and then again, leaving a long beat between the higher range and the lower. She could imagine him facing her, his soft mouth enunciating the notes.

Bum bum bum.

Beat. Drop.

Bum bum bum.

The skinny girl laughed a horsey laugh that set off a nosebleed. Classy. As the girl scrambled in her bag for a tissue and pressed it to her sharp little face, Colleen worked on the tune. It meant something. Heath certainly hadn't hummed this at her over and over again for no reason. She almost recognized the tune but, like her attraction to Heath and her reasons for staying married to him as long as she did, Colleen couldn't bring it to mind.

And, she reminded herself, like everything else about Heath, it didn't matter anymore.

She paid for the drinks, grabbed the wine and the beer, and turned away from the bar without a second glance. Every ounce of her focus went to walking straight, not spilling her drink, not looking over her shoulder to see if Heath followed her. She focused on Bix, who watched her approach with an arched brow and twisted smile.

When Colleen set the drinks down and slipped into her seat, Bix whispered, "You were like ice."

Colleen couldn't quite get her shoulders to relax. "Did you see me?"

"I saw you," Bix said with open admiration. "You didn't even blink. I saw him follow you to the line and I was one hundred percent ready to get up there and kick his pasty ass right over the fence but you didn't need me. You shut that limp-dicked little pansy down with a look that could've withered steel. You were scary!"

Colleen laughed, doubting her, but hoping she was telling the truth.

Bix tapped her cup against Colleen's. "I even saw him try to talk to you. You are an ice princess. I am so proud of you!"

She had to admit she was pretty proud of herself.

The wine went down with increasing ease. Heath and the skinny girl wandered past more than once, collecting a few other equally messed-up young women. All dressed with the same unfortunate flair but, true to Heath's pattern, the girl on his arm managed to look the most . . . whatever that was.

"What do you call that look?" Colleen said, squinting over her plastic cup. "Those thigh-high boots and all that?"

Bix shrugged. "*Pretty Woman* Gets the Millionaire and Stays a Prostitute? The Coke Whore Chronicles?" Bix gave Colleen a look that said she expected to be shushed, to be told she was behaving inappropriately. Instead, Colleen giggled, so Bix went on.

"The Golden Thigh Gap? The Million-Dollar Ham Wallet? The 'I'll Take Blisters for Two Hundred, Alex'?" Colleen knew Bix could and would go on and on, getting louder and louder. She knew she should stop her, but at that moment, with that much wine on the patio of her favorite place on earth, in the presence of Heath, Colleen didn't feel like it. She kind of wanted to make a scene. At the very least, she wanted to hear what Bix could come up with.

Bix didn't disappoint.

"And Heath? I'm looking at that little piece of shit and I'm stunned. How on earth did he get you to marry him? Look at his ass! That's a chick's ass. And not some cheerleader, either. That's a fat girl's ass." Bix didn't pretend to hide her examination of Heath. He occasionally looked their way and smiled as Bix continued her monologue. "And I bet fucking him was a treat. Like getting humped by a pale rabbit. Or getting poked with a dull pencil." Colleen snickered. "That's when he could get it up, right? I'd put money on him pushing rope more times than not."

Heath's skinny girl sidled by them, humming out loud.

Bum bum bum. Bum bum bum.

"The fuck is that song?" Bix asked Colleen, who could feel the old anxiety seeping in around the edges of her laughter. "'The Syphilis Theme Song'?"

Colleen shook her head. "Who cares what it is? Who cares about Heath? Let's watch the race." And so they watched the seventh race and waited for the eighth and final race of the day.

"I have to pee." Colleen stood, not completely steady. Her face felt warm from the sun and her body felt loose from the wine and laughter. Patrick caught her eye. He stood out on the lawn talking with a couple Colleen didn't recognize. Making contacts. Work work work. She'd bet John wasn't working today. Patrick blew her a kiss and then tapped his watch. They'd be leaving soon. That was fine. It was all fine. She felt fine.

She kept an eye out for John in the chaos of the Clubhouse. So many people crowded around the bars and the food window and the betting counter. Funny, she always forgot how crowded it got inside. Why do all these people stay inside on such a gorgeous day? Colleen swayed a little and pretended it was because she'd been bumped. It wasn't like she had any room to go anywhere. The crowd stood nearly shoulder to shoulder, laughing and yelling.

So rowdy. And yet, she noticed with a sense of old-fashioned approval, all the men still had their jackets on. This was Keeneland, after all. Not some saloon.

The line for the ladies' room snaked from the little room of stalls, through the lounge area out front, all the way into the hall. Of course. But Colleen really needed to go, so she took her place and waited. She just waited, thinking about nothing, watching the women around her blend into the busy floral wallpaper.

She had made it to within five feet of the stalls when she heard the familiar cackle.

The room had two large mirrors, one on the wall facing the entrance, one to her right. Women lined up against the mirror to her right and, in the mirror before her, Colleen could see the line stretching out through the door. Just inside the doorway stood Thigh-High Boots and her entourage. One of the other girls had a nosebleed now and was tending to it with a stack of paper napkins. The others laughed and checked their phones, unconcerned with the mess.

Thigh-High caught Colleen's eye in the mirror and sang the tune again. Loudly.

Bum bum bum. Bum bum bum.

Nosebleed fell back against the wall, a wad of napkins lodged in her nose. She looked grumpy. "Why do you keep singing that?"

"It's a great song." Thigh-High showed a lot of teeth and looked past Colleen in the mirror. "Don't you love that song?" *Bum bum bum. Bum bum bum.*

Colleen felt the heat of the girl's stare in the mirror. She could sense the whoosh of silence that rose from the women around her, women unlike Thigh-High and her friends, women who didn't make scenes in public bathrooms. The attention from these women rained down on her like tiny stones, pinging her skin and raising a hot red rash over her arms and neck.

They knew.

They knew what that song meant.

It meant something that everyone in the ladies' room understood. They all understood the implicit insult in those three notes repeated over and over again, how perfectly they applied to Colleen, how unbearably humiliating they were because they were so perfectly applicable.

How doubly humiliating they were because Colleen was the only person in the room, on the planet, who didn't get the joke, who didn't even understand the insult, who just didn't get it.

Again.

As usual.

Colleen never got the joke, never got it right, because as usual Colleen was too fucking stupid, too priggish, too stuck-up.

Needing to be brought down a peg.

Needing to be put back in her fucking place.

Sweat pooled in her hairline before escaping down the sides of her face. In the mirrors, everyone pretended not to stare at her except for Thigh-High. Thigh-High knew the truth. Thigh-High could see the shame on Colleen's face and Colleen could see in the girl's hard eyes that they both knew what was coming.

Thigh-High was going to have to spell it out.

"You know," Thigh-High said, smiling at herself in the mirror, knowing Colleen watched. "That old eighties song by Duran Duran that they always play at the fashion shows." *Bum bum bum.* She put words to the beat. "'Girls on Film.'"

They laughed. Colleen could see it in the mirror, could see their big, horsey teeth. It didn't look like anyone else was laughing—too well-bred for that sort of behavior, weren't they all?—but Colleen could hear it. Could hear barking, braying laughter behind a siren wail that rose up from somewhere deep inside of her.

Like the siren that wailed in the ambulance on the way to the hospital. She had been such a mess. She had made such a mess.

She was going to make another mess.

Vomit shot out of her mouth like an animal escaping. Bits of beef and corn on a tide of brown gravy and white wine, hot and lumpy sailing over her tongue, past her teeth, up her nose, and out onto the dark floral carpet of the Keeneland Clubhouse ladies' lounge.

Women jumped back from the spew. Nobody was that well-bred. Colleen staggered, almost sliding in her mess. An attendant rushed forward with a towel, everyone else stepped back, mortified and repulsed.

Except the Thigh-High gang. They laughed and laughed as Colleen pushed past them. She hit her shoulder hard on the doorframe and stumbled into the crowd, wanting air, wanting out. She went the wrong way, heading into the Clubhouse rather than out, deeper into the crowd rather than toward wide-open fresh air. Oh well, the doors to the patio weren't far. She just had to get past these people, all these people laughing and drinking, blocking her way to the glass doors and the fresh air and Bix and Patrick.

Patrick. Who knew about his girl on film.

Everyone knew about the girl on film.

Her stomach wound up for another pitch of vomit but Colleen hadn't eaten enough to put any weight behind it. Instead, she cramped and grabbed her stomach like she'd been punched. She had been punched so many times the gesture felt horribly familiar and she almost expected to see the usual ribbon of blood dripping from her face onto the floor below.

Not her kitchen floor. Concrete. She was on the patio. Keeneland.

Bix pushed suits aside, her mouth open. Oh no, Bix was laughing, too. That's why she could hear that laughter. Everywhere.

No, Bix wasn't laughing. Bix had her by the shoulders, staring into her eyes. Then glaring past her, behind her, where the laughter was coming from. Then Patrick was there pushing Bix aside, lifting Colleen's chin, brushing her hair off her face. Oh her breath must be horrible. That was all she could think. It was the least worst thing she could think at that moment.

Everyone was staring at her. Oh god.

And then everything fell away at the sound of these words.

"You alright, Colleen?"

Not Patrick's voice. He'd asked her a hundred times, it seemed. Nope, this question came from the one person who wanted the answer to be no.

"You're looking a little green," Heath said, coming up from behind her, Thigh-High and the gang trailing him like giggling smoke. He snapped a picture of her with his phone and held it up. "See? Kind of sweaty. Like you don't feel good. Hey, Pat." He winked at Patrick. "Give me your number. I'll forward this to you. I always knew how to get Colleen's good side."

Like a dream when you try to run but your feet are glued to the sidewalk, Colleen tried to move away from him, to twist or step or lean and so avoid his pale hand that reached out toward her like a scoop. Like a claw. He was grabbing for her ass. He would clutch it and lift it and shove her in whatever direction he chose.

But then something spun her.

A blue wall spun her.

Patrick, sailing past her, enormous and silent until he made contact with Heath. Impact. Solid sounds of flesh on flesh, gasps, grunts, tearing cloth and the unmistakable sound of skull on floor. It sounded different hearing it outside of her own skull but Colleen knew that sound. It sounded a lot better from this side.

Patrick had Heath on the ground. This was no macho bar scuffle. They didn't grapple. Patrick had Heath pinned beneath his knee, one hand holding his throat, the other pounding over and over into the bones of the pale man's face. It only lasted seconds—a half a dozen men tackled Patrick—but it lasted long enough.

The front of Heath was red. His face, his hair, what remained of his shirt, his chest exposed beneath the ripped fabric, the lapels of his plaid jacket. Red streaked with darker red and dappled with the red spray spouting from the hole behind red lips and red teeth.

Everyone shouted except Colleen. They were dragging Patrick from the Clubhouse and someone ran to get towels and ice for Heath. Bix pulled at her arm but Colleen stood there, invisible in the chaos, and watched Heath bleed.

It looked good.

CHAPTER NINE

Bix got Colleen out of the Clubhouse. John was wrestling Patrick away from the crowds as they waited for the valet to pull around. Patrick was almost unrecognizable—his face twisted and red, his posture aggressive, enormous. Colleen had always loved the size of Patrick but she'd never seen him use it to intimidate, never seen him openly wield the power of his mass. She thought he was going to turn on John now, beat the crap out of him. John looked like he thought so, too.

The valet roared up with Patrick's truck. Keeneland didn't play around when it came to banishing problems. It took all of John's strength to get Patrick into the passenger's seat. Colleen hoped John tipped the valet well.

It took longer to fetch Bix's car. Since she and Bix weren't fistfighting, Colleen presumed the valet's urgency had diminished to normal. As a result, they arrived at Colleen's house several minutes after their husbands. When they pulled up in front of the house, they could see that the men were still in the truck's cab. John had survived the ride home, but the fight wasn't over. When Colleen and Bix got out of the car and walked past the truck, they could hear and see the hot argument going on within.

Once inside, Bix poured them both another glass of white wine, which Colleen stupidly drank along with her while their husbands sat outside in the truck.

Summoning a fragment of the sense she had otherwise abandoned that day, Colleen turned down Bix's second pour. Her head swam and her stomach turned and when she heard the front door crash open and Patrick's angry muttering from the front hall, something twisted inside of her.

How many nights in her first marriage had begun with those sounds?

But then, against all reason, her stomach uncoiled. She felt herself grow still inside. A red cartoon imp jabbing a pitchfork into her shoulder whispered in her ear, *We should have drunk more wine when we were married to Heath.*

Patrick stormed through the kitchen, heading for his office at the back of the house. He didn't look over at either woman. He clenched his lips as tightly as his fists.

"Is John still out there?" Bix called after him. She sounded nervous. Fearless Bix, unnerved.

"The fuck should I know?" Patrick growled from the hallway. "Might've taken off. Son of a bitch does what he wants, doesn't he? Fuck everyone else." The office door slammed and Bix flinched.

Completely out of character, Colleen felt calm, if mildly annoyed.

"I'm going to go," Bix whispered. "I think John's still outside. Just give Patrick some space. Let him cool off. He doesn't get angry often but when he does, whew."

"Yeah, thanks." Colleen swallowed her irritation at her friend's unsolicited advice, just nodded coolly and saw her out, pressed the door shut after her.

Look at you, that red imp whispered from her shoulder. *You're tired of taking shit like this, aren't you? Tired of angry husbands stomping around. Tired of being the frightened one. Even Bix is scared, but not you. Not anymore. Have another drink and let's go talk to Patrick.*

She pretended that by not pouring another glass of wine, she retained control of the situation. She didn't give in to her baser desires. She was being rational.

"Patrick?" She pushed open the door to his office. She didn't know what she wanted to say or what she expected to see. Patrick slammed his iPad case shut and glared up at her. No, Colleen caught herself. He didn't glare at her. He glared and then he saw her and his look changed. To what? She still saw anger, black and rolling through his eyes, but when he looked at her that anger gave way just slightly to something else that she couldn't identify. Fear? Guilt?

Shame?

He had taken his jacket off and the cuffs of his white shirt were smeared black and red. His hands were clean. She wondered where he had wiped off Heath's blood.

"I'm glad you did it," she said.

Patrick shook his head, his scarred fingers gripping the edges of the tablet. "That was . . . I shouldn't have handled it like that."

Colleen shrugged. "Maybe not. Maybe there was a civilized way to handle it, but I'm glad you didn't go that way." She stared at his red cuffs. "I wish you could have kept going."

"Don't say that. You don't mean that."

She almost argued with him but stopped herself. She knew where that argument would lead—more talk about the tough life, the life on the streets she would never know, how much violence he'd seen and how much it changed a person and how lucky she was to not have known that life. She wasn't in the mood for it.

"How's John?"

Patrick swore under his breath.

"Was he upset that you messed up his new playmate? Is that what you were arguing about in the car? That he's running around with Heath Seaton?"

He closed his eyes and shook his head. "Colleen, it's complicated."

"Yeah, I bet." She could feel the little imp's pitchfork prodding her. "It's so hard to take the high ground when you're rolling in shit yourself."

He flashed her a look that she recognized, although it looked out of place on Patrick's handsome face.

Fear.

"What does that mean?" he asked.

Why wouldn't she stop talking? Why was she picking this fight with the man she loved? Because she knew he wouldn't hurt her? That was stupid, immature. She should throw her arms around his neck, kiss him and thank him for loving her, for defending the honor that had been so badly damaged. She should hold him and forgive him for his violence even while she thanked him for it. She should love him like he loved her.

Instead, she kept talking.

"I mean it's hard to judge your best friend for whatever he's doing with Heath Seaton. We all know they're doing something together, right? We're not pretending that something isn't up, right? Is that why you guys are fighting? Is John going out on his own, into some 'business venture' with Heath?" She made a show of air quotes and put little effort into keeping the nastiness out of her tone.

Patrick shook his head and started to speak, but Colleen cut him off.

"It's tough, right? I mean, you want to beat the shit out of Heath Seaton, if not for what he did to me then at least for whatever disaster he's dragging John into. Because everyone knows you two always have each other's back. But then you don't really have a leg to stand on, since you're in bed with Heath's brother-in-law. And Arlen Henderschott— and it boggles the mind to realize this—is an even bigger piece of shit than Heath. It must be so awkward between you and John, fighting over who gets to make the bigger mistake. Good luck with that."

"Are you done?" The edges of his lips were white.

"Are you?" She folded her arms and leaned against the doorframe. "Are you done doing business with Arlen?"

He fell back in his chair. "You want me to stop doing business with the Gables Medical Center. Just pack it up and throw that money away. Just turn down the business, turn down the medical care they provide for Green Fields, because the CEO happens to be married to someone who is related to your ex-husband."

"Yes."

"Unbelievable."

"No, not unbelievable, Patrick. You talk so much about how you don't fit in here, how much you appreciate me giving you and John entrée into Lexington society, like it's some kind of diamond-encrusted Narnia with money trees you can just pluck from." She pushed away from the door and marched to his desk. "You and Bix and John are always telling me how I don't understand where you came from. Well, you don't understand where I came from.

"I come from a world where people like Arlen Henderschott and Dilly Seaton Henderschott and Heath Seaton think they are above the law, that the morals of the world don't apply to them. They think that they can fuck people and hurt people and ruin people." Her voice broke on that but she wouldn't stop. "They think they can just throw money at whatever comes up and that the world will just give them a pass. And every time you do business with them, you let them buy a little bit more of you."

"So what about you?" Patrick's voice was flat. "You took money from them."

"Yeah, but I didn't need it."

"Ah." His hands gripped the edge of the desk, spots of that red anger reappearing on his cheeks. "But I do need it."

"No you don't."

"Because I'm married to you?"

"Yes."

"No. That's not how this works, Colleen."

"Why not? No, don't tell me." She waved him back into his chair. "It's because you're a man and you came from nothing and you're not going to just live off your wife, right? That's beneath you. That's undignified. That makes you less than a man, right?"

She couldn't stop herself. It felt good to say these things, even though she knew she would regret them. But like one drink too many, she kept her eye on the buzz with no thought to the hangover.

"Well, let me give you a little advice, okay? You turn to me for fashion advice and to ask about which fork to use. We'll just put this on the list of insights." She leaned on his desk with both hands. "You're probably right to not stop working with Arlen right now because, you see, now that you've smashed up Heath's pretty face, Heath's going to want to sue you, if not press charges. But Arlen will magnanimously agree to repair Heath's face and cover all the medical bills so as not to bring the police into it. Of course, Arlen will let you know that those bills aren't going to pay themselves, that someone has to foot the bill. And so, before you know it, you'll be working for Arlen Henderschott for free. You and John can rename your business—"

"Stop it."

She almost kept going but then reconsidered. He didn't yell. He didn't use his size to intimidate her. The look in his eyes wasn't angry, wasn't hurt, wasn't fearful. It was cold, but somehow that cold didn't seem directed at her. He looked disconnected.

"Don't say whatever it was you were going to say, Colleen. You're drunk. I'm angry. It's been a long day. I have to fly to Indianapolis tomorrow. We can talk when I get back."

CHAPTER TEN

Sunday, October 4

Colleen woke up a little after eleven. Her left eyelashes stuck together, glued with sleep, and it took all of her strength to blink them open. Her lips and tongue burned with dehydration and even the smallest movements sent panicked alarms through her stomach and spine.

This felt like more than a hangover. This felt like the flu.

But she knew it was a hangover. White wine. Sunshine. Day drinking.

And stress.

Fragments of yesterday's misfortunes popped up in her memory. Oh god, she'd vomited on the floor at Keeneland. Heath, beaten to a bloody pulp. The Thigh-High gang. Oh god. Talking about filming her.

She tried to glue her eyes shut once more, to drive herself deep into the mattress in the hopes that this one time her bed would act as a time machine and give her a chance for a total do-over. No luck. The taste in her mouth acted as the hook upon which all memories hung. Vomit. Chaos. Shame.

Not really in that order though, were they?

She turned her head to the right, knowing what she would see. Patrick's side of the bed lay untouched. With a whimper, she pulled herself up to sitting, grabbing her skull to keep it from blowing to pieces. Where had Patrick gone last night?

Her memory stayed fixated on the fight between Patrick and Heath. No, not a fight, a beating. She replayed it over and over in her mind. Heath never got a single blow in. Heath, who had never spared her his fists when they were married, never got a single swing in. She poked around inside her mind, lifting up the blanket of shame and humiliation that lay over the entire expanse of yesterday, and found little caches of pleasure at Heath's beatdown. Pride. There was no hiding it from herself even if she'd wanted to. Some primitive part of her was proud of Patrick, her man, for beating down an enemy. He was pure rage and might. Gorillas with rocks and logs, smashing each other over jungle territory, over mating rights.

It hadn't exactly ended in pure animal lust though, had it?

The things she'd said to Patrick last night, the way she'd needled him. She'd wanted to make a point and what did she wind up with? A hangover and an empty bed.

She didn't want to get out of this bed. She especially didn't want to go down to the kitchen. That was their place, the place they shared pieces of themselves every bit as intimate as they did in the bedroom.

The house felt different without Patrick in it, bigger and smaller at the same time. Strange, since he hadn't been living here a year. The little brick row house had been in Colleen's family for generations. She'd inherited it from her aunt. Colleen and her sisters had lived in this house on and off through college and afterwards. When Colleen had finished at Wellesley, she and her younger sister, Moira, had lived here together.

Now Moira lived in London, running her own environmental consulting firm. Their older sister, Isabel, was raising her four boys in Austin, Texas. Colleen had moved out of the house when she married

Heath. For four years the house had been rented to students and lawyers and young families.

When Colleen had gotten out of the hospital, without a marriage and without a spleen, she'd known where she wanted to go. But first she had to go back to the house she had shared with Heath, though *share* could be used only very, very loosely. When she came through that front door, she'd seen blood on the carpet, the knocked-over table, the broken wine bottles, and the belt. She'd seen the dirty footprints the paramedics had left behind. The telephone someone had been considerate enough to return to its cradle, the phone she had begged to use, the phone she had spent the very last drop of her strength to crawl toward after Heath had finished with her, after he had exhausted his vast reservoir of rage and degradation.

She saw it all and knew she would take very little with her to her family's narrow brick home just north of Lexington's historic district. As luck would have it, it was between tenants. Alyssa had urged Colleen to press charges against Heath, and when Colleen wouldn't, the attorney had leveraged the damage and disgrace Heath had brought down into an obscenely costly divorce settlement.

At the time, Colleen hadn't cared about any of it. She couldn't bear to. She just wanted it all to go away, to retreat to the yellow bedroom of her younger years.

When she moved back in, the bedroom was no longer yellow. Renters had damaged the built-in shelves in the living room and someone had replaced the bathroom tile with ugly vinyl stick-on squares. These small cosmetic scars and changes only strengthened her resolve to move in. The house needed her as badly as she needed it.

There were things she wanted from her marriage house—keepsakes and heirlooms she couldn't bear to leave behind. The doctors had told Colleen that, after her splenectomy, she needed to be careful about any heavy lifting. She would have laughed if she could remember how.

Nobody needed to remind Colleen to be careful about anything any-more. Caution had been beaten into her very marrow.

So when it came time to hire a mover to do her heavy lifting, Colleen passed over any mover recommended to her, anyone used by friends or family, any business connected in any way to her old life. She wouldn't take the chance of trusting anything, especially her privacy, to anyone who might have known the truth of her disastrous marriage and shameful divorce.

That's when she found the ad for Macaroni Brothers in a free local paper. She called the number and a woman answered. Bix, she now knew. The woman had peppered her with blunt, impatient questions about square footage and types of trucks and estimated delivery win-dows. Colleen had nearly hung up until a man picked up on the exten-sion. He sounded happy and easygoing. He told her not to worry, that they could give her a free estimate and that he was sure they could work something out. That man was John Mulroney.

But it was Patrick McElroy she saw first in person. He stepped into the mostly empty living room quietly, carefully, as if he feared he would accidentally break something. Colleen's first gut reaction to his presence had been fear. Her brain immediately informed her that she would never survive a beating from a man of his size. Then John came in, all smiles and easy manners. They came to a reasonable price, the few items were moved, and Patrick McElroy took his first steps into her family home.

"I can fix that," were the first words he spoke to her directly. He had carried in a box of Irish china that had survived when most of her other dishware had been destroyed. He pointed to a pantry door that didn't close properly. "As soon as we're done here," he said, "I'll reattach that door so it closes. It'll only take a minute or two."

When he replaced the pantry door hinges, Colleen noticed the scars on his hands. When he replaced a light fixture he had knocked loose in the foyer, she realized how brown his eyes were. When he left his card and told her he would be happy to repair the screens on the back porch, Colleen noticed that, despite his size and obvious strength, Patrick McElroy didn't frighten her.

A month later, she hired him to fix the screens. A month after that, he returned to patch her roof and repair her gutters. Four years of renters had damaged the old house and four months after moving back in, Patrick McElroy was painting her old bedroom the yellow she remembered.

Three months after that, he visited the bedroom for more pleasurable reasons, and two months after that, Colleen understood how much repair work Patrick had truly done.

Now they shared the yellow bedroom. They ate off the Irish china and stored groceries in the pantry with the door that stayed shut. Patrick never knocked that light fixture loose again. Everything should have been fine.

But here she was, the day after the opening of Keeneland, alone and hungover, the taste of the words she had spoken as bitter as the vomit she had spewed. What worried her wasn't that she had said those things to the man she loved. And she did love Patrick. God, she loved him in ways she hadn't known she was capable of. Even when she was angry, especially when she was angry, she felt her love for him like a limb that had suddenly grown from the center of her, something strong and muscular that she'd never realized she'd been missing.

What worried her wasn't that she would say such things to a man she loved so fiercely. What worried her was that even now, after her anger had evaporated along with the alcohol, she could feel the truth in what she had said.

John involved with Heath.

Patrick involved with Arlen.

Both of them dancing with the devil.

CHAPTER ELEVEN

Monday, October 5

Colleen made her way across Market Street, watching for traffic and wet leaves. It had rained all day Sunday, giving her a perfect excuse to spend the day moving from the bed to the couch and back to the bed. She didn't want to think about the nasty things she had said to Patrick. She didn't want to think about him flying with those words in his heart. So she didn't think about anything but sleeping and listening to the leaves blowing around in the fall rain.

She'd gotten a text from Alyssa before bed.

Coffee tomorrow? 2:30 Gratz Park? I've got some info on that list— weird. Let's talk.

That didn't sound good.

But however bad it might be, Colleen still looked forward to seeing her old roommate. That's how she would refer to Alyssa from now on, she decided—her old roommate, rather than her attorney. The divorce was over. They'd been friends before the divorce. They were still friends. It was time to focus on her life now, to change her inner monologue. Words matter.

Like the words she had jabbed at Patrick Saturday night.

Oh well. One thing at a time.

Gratz Park was lovely, as usual. Rain or shine, regardless of the season, Colleen loved the little park. Just one city block, it was flanked on three sides by the charming colored row houses of the historic district with Transylvania University at its north. That was the direction Alyssa would be coming from, Colleen knew, since she was delivering a lecture on Women in Law for a senior class seminar. Colleen found a sunny spot by the low fountain at the north end of the park and waited.

Traffic buzzed through the narrow streets. Although Transylvania enrolled a fraction of the students that UK pulled in on the other side of town, the neighborhood felt busy when school was in session. The historic district clung to its charm with narrow brick streets that wound their way toward the busy downtown. She'd been lucky to find parking. She watched several cars circling the park hoping to get as fortunate, then spotted Alyssa waving from across the street, holding up two paper cups, working them like signaling flags to stop traffic long enough to run across the street. One driver dared to beep his horn and Alyssa treated him to a girlish curtsy without spilling a drop.

"I hope you don't mind the generic brew," she said, handing Colleen a cup. "I've got to be back at the seminar in twenty minutes and I'm in meetings all day and court tomorrow."

"I appreciate it, but this isn't a rush. We can talk later on in the week."

Alyssa focused on getting the lid off her cup and taking a sip. "I don't want to wait. I want to talk to you first. But have you tasted this coffee? The woman in the dean's office makes it every morning. It's weak and bitter and I'm absolutely addicted to it. I hope you didn't want cream or sugar. I don't want to ruin the delicious horror of whatever she does to this stuff."

Colleen took a sip and tried not to grimace. "An acquired taste?"

"Stick with it. Let's walk." She linked her free arm in Colleen's just like she used to do at St. Agatha's, when they would hurry across campus, their heads together, making plans for whatever trouble they were brewing. Colleen liked the feel of their shoulders bumping.

They turned the corner and walked the length of the low, stone Bodley-Bullock House that ran almost half the length of the park. Wet leaves coated the sidewalk, brown and yellow and glossy with rain. She wondered if Alyssa would notice if she discreetly poured out the coffee as they walked.

"So this list," Alyssa said. "John had this list on his phone?"

"Yes, and I think Heath sent it."

The attorney let out an unhappy sigh. "Well, anything Heath is involved with is probably unpleasant, but you aren't sure Heath has anything to do with this. What worries me is John's involvement. Do you know if Patrick knows anything about this list?"

"I haven't asked him. I asked him about John doing business—or whatever they're calling it—with Heath, and that was enough to start a fight." Colleen caught her friend's curious glance. "It didn't help that I used that discussion to launch into a tirade about him doing business with Arlen Henderschott."

"How did he take that?"

"It probably would have gone more smoothly had I not resorted to phrases like *rolling in shit* and *turning into Arlen's bitch.*"

"Ouch."

"Yeah, it turned into quite a fight. It seems I'm a mean white-wine drunk."

Alyssa snorted. "You know what they say. Liquor don't lie. Just because you didn't put it tactfully doesn't mean you weren't telling the truth."

"Does this list have something to do with Arlen? Or Gables?"

"Not that I can see." They turned right at the corner. A cluster of students posed for a group photo at that end of the park, the stately steps of the ArtsPlace their backdrop. A silver Escalade honked at them for blocking traffic. Alyssa guided Colleen into the grass to sidestep the photographer. "This list is weird. Like I said, the names are common and there aren't enough names to be absolutely certain what the focus is. I mean, if we had twenty names, maybe we could find patterns or groups. We might be able to eliminate certain possibilities and narrow down which people the names refer to."

"What do you mean?" Colleen asked. "Are they aliases or something?"

"I mean, do you know how many Karen Biases there are in Kentucky? And Scott Burnses? Don't get me started on the Kilgores or Smiths. The only ones who have no duplicates are Catielyn Miller and Luda Wayne Napier, because of the unusual spellings. Assuming they're not misspelled. Which I'm kind of hoping they are, so that they're not the constant on which we focus the group."

Colleen really didn't want to ask this question. "Why not?"

"Because the only Catielyn Miller we could find is thirteen years old and Luda Wayne Napier is fifteen." She let that sink in as they turned the corner once more. "I harbor a lot of bad feelings toward Heath Seaton. I don't think a lot more of John Mulroney, but even I would hesitate to accuse either of them of involving children in whatever it is they're doing."

"What about the other names?"

"The other names take the discussion in a thousand directions. For initial simplicity we kept the search within current Kentucky residents. Currently there are seven Karen Biases on record. But one of them stood out. She died in April." Colleen's breath caught and Alyssa nodded. "Yep. She OD'd on pills. She'd been turning tricks for pills for over a year. She became even more interesting to me when I found out that before she died, she had been in jail with an Elizabeth Smith, another name on the list, another Oxy-hooker."

"That sounds more like something Heath would know about."

"My thoughts exactly. But none of the other names on the list have records for anything more serious than speeding tickets and a DUI. Which brings me back to Catielyn Miller and what she has in common with a dead pillhead."

"Do I want to know this?"

Alyssa shrugged. "It may be nothing. Like I said, these names aren't unique and you don't even know if it's limited to Kentucky, but so far, with just preliminary searching, each one of these names has been on the roster of the DCBS." She looked at Colleen to see if she understood. "The Department for Community Based Services. You know, otherwise known as the foster care system."

"Oh shit."

"Yeah." They stood for a moment watching the silver Escalade that had honked earlier stop beside a parking space much too small for it. "Good luck with that, buddy," Alyssa muttered and pulled Colleen along. "Now bear in mind, the Department for Community Based Services is a big umbrella, covering everything from foster care to family court. Plus, John does work with Green Fields. You've told me that kids have stayed in touch with him and Patrick over the years. It could be completely harmless."

"Unless Heath is involved."

"Unless Heath is involved," Alyssa agreed. "Just having Heath in the vicinity of children is grounds for endangering a minor."

"Is Catielyn Miller at Green Fields now? Were any of those people there?"

"Catielyn is currently with a foster family. That's all I could find out and that was just by sheer luck. As for the others, those records are sealed. It took a few favors to find out about the DCBS roster. I suppose I could find out where specifically they were housed but that would be a lot of work for something that might not add up to anything. Would you look at that guy?"

She nodded toward the silver Escalade that had driven up over the sidewalk on West Third Street, nearly hitting a group of students waiting to cross over to campus. They couldn't see the driver behind the SUV's tinted windows but they could see one of the students yelling at him as she made her way to the other side of the street.

Colleen pulled Alyssa toward the grass, giving the idiot and his Escalade a wide berth. "So what do you think? You were worried enough to want to talk to me in person about it. Do you think this list is something to worry about?"

Alyssa tossed her coffee cup into a nearby garbage can. "I don't know, Coll. The dead hooker and her cellmate both being on the list looks bad, but let's be honest. Pills aren't exactly exotic in Kentucky. The odds are if you make a long enough list, you're going to find some drug users on it. The foster care thing has the potential to be disturbing, but John does work with at risk kids. So does your husband." She squeezed Colleen's arm. "Which is why I suggest that you talk with him. Nobody is closer to John Mulroney than Patrick McElroy."

Colleen nodded. "I feel stupid. I feel terrible for the things I said to Patrick before he left. I feel like I'm turning into Bix, blowing things out of proportion, flipping out just to hear my own voice."

"Trust me, I will stop you long before you turn into Bix Mulroney." Alyssa unhooked her arm from Colleen's where they stood at the corner they had started from. "The list is probably nothing. Bix is probably stirring up some kind of drama. She knows how you feel about Heath so she's probably overplaying the connection between him and John. Having a drink with someone does not make you coconspirators."

"You're right," Colleen said although she had little faith in anyone being uncontaminated by contact with Heath Seaton. "I'm sorry I wasted your time."

"Don't be ridiculous," Alyssa said. "You know I'm happy to do anything for you. I'm proud to be the personal counsel of Mad Dog Dooley." She kissed Colleen on the cheek. "Ask Patrick about the list.

See what he says. Try to do it when you're not drunk, Mad Dog. If you get more names, if you find out anything that you think can narrow down the explanation, send it to me. I'm happy to help. Just promise me you won't ever send Bix Mulroney to my office."

Colleen laughed. "I give you my Mad Dog word of honor."

Colleen headed down West Third Street as Alyssa crossed over back to campus. The sun broke through the last of the clouds and she had to squint at the light reflecting off the wet leaves. Alyssa was right—Bix was probably dragging her into something just for the drama. Bix loved to fight with John. All those gross things she had told her about the STDs. Colleen grimaced. They were almost as gross as the coffee Alyssa had brought.

She dumped the cold coffee into the grass and crushed the paper cup. On the corner across the street sat an open-wire garbage can. Mounted dead center on its side was a "Do Not Litter" sign.

Colleen paused, feeling a little stupid as she squinted across the street at the sign, rolling the wadded-up cup in her right hand. There was no getting away from it, though. The sign was the right size, the right height—the catcher's glove, calling for knee-high smoke. She looked both ways to see if anyone was paying her any attention. The coast was clear. She switched her purse to her left shoulder and the crushed cup to her left hand. One, two quick windmills with her right arm to loosen the shoulder. Feet together on the rubber, hands waist high before her. Right hand gripping the ball now, rolling it inside her glove, finding the seams. Lock on target, cock glove and ball at right hip, stride and windmill and fire.

The missile pinged off the left side of the can and ricocheted into the street.

"Not bad, Mad Dog," she whispered to herself. With a laugh, she ran to pick up the cup and deposit it into the garbage can on the way to her car.

CHAPTER TWELVE

She was still laughing as she pulled her ringing phone from her bag.

"Patrick?"

"Colleen? Hey, it's me." She could hear traffic and machinery in his background. "I wanted to call yesterday but I just thought maybe you would need some time."

She climbed into the car to hear him better. "Patrick, I'm so sorry about those things I said. I should never have—"

"No, no, don't say that, Colleen. You should never apologize to me. God." He sighed and Colleen could hear the exhaustion in his voice. "I'm like a broken record. Every day I'm apologizing for losing my temper. I don't want to be that man." His voice broke.

"Patrick, no. It was stupid. I'd had too much to drink. And I really was glad you beat the crap out of Heath. I know that's adolescent, but I won't apologize for it and neither should you."

"It's not that simple, Colleen."

The sadness in his tone made her heart ache. Patrick was always so hard on himself and now she had just added to it. She wanted to say something to make him understand that he had nothing to prove to her, that he was enough just as he was. Before she could come up with anything to say, a horn blared outside her window.

"You have got to be kidding me," she spoke to the reflection in her rearview.

"What?" Patrick asked.

"No, not you. It's this stupid Escalade. It's been driving around the park like a lunatic and now it's waiting for me to pull out of my parking spot. Hold on." She rolled down the window and waved the big vehicle on, but the driver just honked once more.

"Where are you?"

"I'm at Gratz Park. I was meeting Alyssa." Colleen hit speaker and put the key in the ignition. The Escalade driver was clearly not going to give up anytime soon.

Patrick said nothing for a long moment. "You met with your attorney?"

"Yeah." Colleen pulled out into traffic, giving the driver behind her a "what the hell?" gesture. Then she realized how this must sound to Patrick, her meeting with her divorce attorney after their second fight of the week. "It was just something I had her checking on. We just met for a quick coffee."

She heard his sigh of relief. "You would tell me, wouldn't you? I mean, if you've had enough. If I've gone too far. You would tell me, right? Give me a chance to talk to you?"

"Oh, Patrick. It's nothing like that. It *won't* be anything like that. You were mad. I was mad." She wanted to get through to him but construction was snarling up traffic and she had to keep her eyes on the road. "Let's talk about this when you get home. When are you getting home?"

"This evening. But I have to fly out tonight at nine."

"Tonight?" She hurried to make it through a yellow light. "You didn't have anything on the calendar. Where are you going tonight?"

She knew his answer by his hesitation. "Back to Indianapolis."

"Another Gables job."

"Yeah. Look, Colleen, I know you hate this and I can see your point, but you have to give me some time. I promise you, I'm building something here and I just need you to understand." The noises in the background dropped off, like he had closed himself into a quiet room, and Colleen could hear the urgency in his voice. "Right now, things are a mess. There's some stuff going on that I don't want you involved in. Things that we just have to work out on our own. But I promise you, Colleen, we'll get on the other side of this. I just need you to give me some time. To believe in me."

Colleen cleared the construction zone and headed north for home. "This thing you have to get to the other side of, does it involve John?" Silence. "It does, doesn't it? It's about whatever he and Heath are doing."

"I'm taking care of it."

"Are you, Patrick? Or are you covering for him? Again? I know you two are close but if he's going off the rails, you need to decide how far you're willing to go with him." She wanted to tell him about John's list that included the name of two hookers, one of whom was dead, and two teenage girls. It didn't seem like the kind of topic to broach while navigating traffic.

"I'm taking care of it, Colleen."

Traffic thinned as she headed away from downtown. Still, this wasn't a conversation to have over speakerphone. "We need to talk about this when you get home."

"Yeah, I know. We will. Just give me some time. Let me get this job done."

Their good-byes weren't chilly but they had had warmer send-offs. Colleen tossed the phone into the passenger's seat and settled back to drive. She didn't have anywhere to go; she just felt like driving. What would Patrick do if John were to get into legal trouble? It was one thing to bail a friend out of a jam. It was quite another to let someone drag you into something illegal and maybe dangerous.

Why was John talking with Heath? Why would Heath send him a list of names and what kind of "deals" were they talking about? And the girls. The presence of two hookers on the list was bad enough, but thirteen- and fifteen-year-old girls?

Whatever it was, surely this wasn't the direction John wanted to take the business. Was he really taking Macaroni Brothers Freight to some criminally horrible level? Colleen couldn't believe it. John was a lot of things—mostly a drunk—but the idea that he could be working with Heath Seaton to—what? Lure young girls into a hard-partying lifestyle? Into prostitution? It just seemed too terrible, too lurid.

More importantly, it seemed like a lot of work. Colleen obviously lacked Bix's knowledge of "running whores" or whatever she had called it, but she imagined an operation like that would surely take a lot of work. Patrick was the Macaroni Brother who did most of the work; John just offered what he called "moral support." And Heath Seaton had never worked a day in his life.

She was missing something. Maybe Patrick already knew what was going on. He said he was trying to build something, that something was going on with John. Maybe that's why he was working for Arlen Henderschott. Maybe it had something to do with Heath.

My god, Colleen thought. Was John in trouble with Heath Seaton? Had he run up some kind of debt or done something that couldn't be undone? Was that why Patrick and John had been fighting lately? Visions of young dead women turning tricks for pills grabbed for her attention. Had Colleen been on the mark when she accused Patrick of being in Arlen's debt? Was he already working to pay off some trouble John was in?

This was pointless. She was making herself crazy over something that was probably nothing more than a missent text and Bix's overly graphic imagination. Alyssa didn't think there was anything to worry about.

No, that wasn't true.

Alyssa told her to talk with Patrick about it. And Patrick had put her off to talk later.

Colleen nearly missed the turnoff to head back toward home. In her musings, she had driven far north of Lexington, taking narrower and narrower roads through green fields and golf course country. She wasn't far off course—she knew generally where she was—but this driving wasn't doing her any good. It gave her too much time to think and her thoughts weren't doing her any favors.

Early afternoon on Monday in the suburbs, she had the road pretty much to herself. She knew I-64 would get her home more quickly, but she decided to stick to the small roads. She turned on the radio, flipping through the channels for something to sing to. She found a Pink song on 104.5 and started to sing along.

That's when she saw the Escalade in the rearview mirror.

It didn't register at first. Colleen didn't know much about cars and one SUV looked pretty much like any other, but Escalades were larger than most and the silver color stood out. Could it be the same guy from Gratz Park? It seemed impossible. She was miles from the park and certainly not on a popular route through the area.

The driver had the visor down and Colleen couldn't make out his face. The big vehicle stayed two car lengths behind her. How long had it been back there?

She sped up a little. The Escalade kept pace. Same thing when she slowed down.

Never closer. Never farther.

A hot flush of anxiety flooded up from her stomach. This was nothing, she told herself. A weird coincidence. It probably wasn't even an Escalade—but she didn't believe that. As little as she knew about cars, even she could recognize the enormous grille with the large chrome emblem in the center.

You're in the suburbs, she reasoned. There are a lot of showy cars out here, people who still think bigger is better. This can't be the only Escalade in Lexington.

It pulled up closer to her.

Her four-door Camry wasn't a small car by any means but, as it approached, the Escalade dwarfed it, looming up behind her like a chrome grille wall. Why didn't it pass her? There was no traffic coming from the other direction. Whoever was driving could easily see past her lower car. If they weren't passing her, it was because they wanted to stay behind her.

They wanted her to see them.

They wanted to scare her.

It was working. If there was one thing Colleen could recognize, it was bullying tactics. A raised fist or a too-close bumper, both worked the same way. A show of force, a show of strength, the clear message: "I am bigger than you and you must bend to me."

"What?" Colleen screamed into the rearview mirror. "What do you want?" Her knuckles ached from gripping the wheel so tightly.

Then the Escalade pulled out to pass her.

Colleen let out a shaky breath, feeling stupid and relieved and stupid at how relieved she felt. When would she lose this fear of imminent danger? When would she stop reading aggression into every little thing?

Hoping to regain some semblance of normalcy, and just in case the driver had seen her screaming into the rearview, Colleen glanced over at the big vehicle as it pulled alongside her. She hoped her smile looked casual and not as rattled and insane as she felt. When the tinted window rolled down, she even thought about trying a friendly wave.

Then she saw the driver.

Heath.

It took a second for her conscious mind to recognize him through the swelling and bruising but her instinctive mind saw the danger right away. Adrenaline dumped into her body and, in her shock, her foot slipped off the pedal, her hands forgot the wheel.

It only took a second but that was enough time for her car to slow down and the Escalade to pull ahead slightly. Colleen snapped to quickly, grabbing the wheel. She almost punched the accelerator but what good would that do? Was she going to race him? Where? What did he want?

She got her answer when the Escalade swerved suddenly in front of her, cutting her off and forcing her to slide into the gravel on the shoulder. Her car swerved but clung to the road. In front of her, the big SUV swerved right and then left, then righted itself, driving straight down the center of the road, straddling the yellow line.

What could she do? She couldn't pass him. Ditches on either side of the road would make a three-point turn slow and almost impossible. And as hard as it was to believe, two decades of driving etiquette were hard to break, even when terrified. It took all of her control to stop the car in the middle of the road—to just stop. Ahead of her, the Escalade did the same, its brake lights shining at her like the eyes of some demon.

What now? Through her fear, Colleen realized how stupid this standoff was. What was Heath going to do? He was just trying to scare her. Well you did it, you piece of shit, she thought. You scared me. Now what?

The red brake lights were joined by glaring white lights. He had put the Escalade in reverse. This couldn't be happening. Was Heath going to ram her in reverse? Drive her backward? Into what? A two-foot ditch? It would hurt; the air bag would deploy. It wouldn't kill her but it would immobilize her long enough for Heath to get his hands on her out here on this empty road with no witnesses, no help. She jammed her own car into reverse. If he was going to hit her, she was going to take the impact out of it.

His brake lights dimmed. Tires screeched and the rear of the Escalade roared toward her. She floored her Toyota and flew backward along the straight, flat road. There was no point in looking behind her. If she hit something, the Escalade would roll right over her.

Heath was finally going to kill her.

She couldn't believe the day had come.

They hadn't gone a hundred yards, although it felt like a thousand miles, when the Escalade swerved to the left and accelerated. Before she could figure out how to adjust besides making sure it didn't rake that side of the Camry, the big silver beast pulled alongside her, both of them speeding along in reverse.

Colleen stomped the brakes and the Escalade flew past her. A breath. A beat. The Escalade stopped, too. Heath flipped the visor up so she could see him through the windshield. He smiled. Those small, even teeth looked even whiter against his blood-bruised lips.

She couldn't beat him. His vehicle was faster and bigger than hers. His Escalade would crush her Toyota. There was nobody on the road and nothing she could do. The paralysis that started in her neck and trailed down to her fingertips felt almost comfortable in its familiarity. She relaxed.

When the Escalade engine revved, she closed her eyes.

She didn't even flinch when she heard the scraping and clattering.

Then he was gone. She opened her eyes and could see the Escalade disappearing in front of her.

She was fine. The car hadn't moved. The windows weren't broken. The air bag hadn't deployed. What had she heard?

The side-view mirror was gone.

The son of a bitch had done all of that just to take off her mirror. Just to show her he could. Colleen felt sweat behind her knees and under her arms and in the small of her back as she dissolved into tears.

She didn't know how long she sat there. She felt limp and wet with flop sweat and tears when she finally opened the car door. Nobody had driven by. Nobody had stopped to help. She climbed out on unsteady legs. Ahead of the car lay her side mirror. The glass wasn't even cracked.

Wires hung out the bottom and tiny fragments of the plastic casing had given way, but it seemed like the whole thing was designed to just pop off.

A convenient way to minimize damage should your ex-husband decide to terrorize you.

Colleen considered not touching the mirror. Would this be some sort of evidence? Could the police tell what had happened from the placement of her car and the placement of the mirror? There were tire marks on the road from where they had swerved. She had left a patch of rubber when she'd slammed on her brakes, but would that be enough for evidence? Would the police believe her?

Would they care?

A hysterical woman who claimed her ex-husband wanted to kill her but had succeeded only in knocking off her side mirror? She could imagine them, the police, taking the report, hiding their smirks, asking her if she had insurance, telling her to call her husband. She could just hear them using the words *little lady*.

The Seatons had made all of the evidence of Heath's abuse disappear. Even her missing spleen hadn't been enough to catch the eye of justice. A popped-off mirror certainly wouldn't bring down the long arm of the law.

Colleen gathered up the mirror and got back into the car. She cradled the broken thing in her lap like an injured pet. The engine hummed as she just sat there in the middle of the road, thinking nothing. Feeling nothing.

She had to do something. She should tell Patrick. That's what the cops would tell her to do. "Tell your husband, honey," she could hear them in her head. And then what? What would Patrick do if she told him what had happened?

He would believe her. Of that she was sure. He would believe her in an instant and then she would see that anger again. A shiver moved through her at the thought of seeing that rage on Patrick's beautiful face again. Was the shiver from fear or was it a thrill?

Oh the violence Patrick would rain down on Heath, making the first beating seem like a handshake. Patrick had it in him. She knew he did. But then what? Whatever universal justice Patrick brought to bear on Heath would be co-opted by the corruption of the Seatons. His violence would be useless against their money and influence. It would damn him.

She would lose Patrick to them. He couldn't know about this.

Colleen needed to get out of the road. She couldn't sit here forever. Surely somebody drove down this road occasionally but she couldn't make herself move. She wanted to talk to someone. It occurred to her that Heath might not be done with her. He might be waiting down the road in a truly hidden place, to get it right. To take it all the way to the finish.

She found her phone and called Alyssa. Voice mail. She didn't leave a message. What was she going to say? "In case I'm dead, Heath did it. Talk to you soon, I hope!" Then Alyssa would worry and ask her questions and want her to call the police even though they both knew how futile that would be. Poor Colleen, the victim again.

"Fuck," she said to herself. It felt good so she said it again. She wanted to be mad. She wanted to strike out. She wanted someone to see her righteous outrage.

Bix.

Bix wouldn't cluck and advise her to be careful. Bix would get pissed with her. Bix would let her rage and storm and agree with her about what a piece of shit her ex-husband was.

Bix picked up on the second ring. Colleen didn't waste time with any pleasantries, not even a hello. As soon as she heard the other woman's voice, the story roared out of her, fat with profanity and rage. She gripped the broken mirror as she spoke, her voice getting louder with every second. Bix said nothing. She just let her talk and talk, getting out every detail.

Colleen ended with "I can't tell Patrick."

"You're god damned right you can't. Patrick will tear his fucking head off and that's just the start of it."

Colleen felt something bloom inside of her. Bix understood.

"Come to the hangar. Bring the mirror. We'll figure this out."

CHAPTER THIRTEEN

The long road of low industrial buildings looked as abandoned as the road on which Heath had terrorized her. Where did everyone go on a Monday afternoon? Colleen wondered as Bix waved her into the open truck bay door.

"Is John here?" Colleen asked through the open car window.

"Hell no. Why would he be? Just because it's a workday and he's part owner?" Bix flicked her cigarette out onto the driveway. "Don't park there. Come on back deeper." She guided Colleen forward, through a narrow alley of racks and pallets. Colleen held her breath, trusting Bix to keep her from smashing into or running over anything. She couldn't imagine how she would ever back out of this spot. As it was, she barely had room to open the door and wriggle out of the cab.

"One of the vans is missing from outside," Colleen said, her voice echoing within the hangar, the absence of Patrick's plane making the space feel even more cavernous. "Maybe John is out on a job."

Bix snorted. "A blow job, maybe. Let me see your mirror." Colleen leaned back in to grab the broken mirror from the passenger seat then shut the door and walked it back to Bix behind the car. She examined the exposed rubber gasket and dangling wires. "Looks like it popped off pretty clean. They're built to do that since they don't fold in like truck mirrors. Saves the car from any serious body damage."

"I guess that's good news."

Bix looked up at her. Colleen supposed she still had shock and trauma written all over her face because Bix lunged for her, grabbing her in a tight bear hug. She had a good five inches on Colleen, which meant her face easily fit into the warm privacy of the other woman's neck. Colleen could see why the kids liked this so much. Bix felt huge and strong, like being protected by a mother bear. She hugged her back and let Bix rock her back and forth for a minute.

"Are you sure you're okay?"

Colleen nodded against her.

"That flaming piece of shit deserves the beatdown your husband would hand him. I have half a mind to hand Pat a wrench and tell him what happened, just wind him up and let him go."

Colleen pulled away. "I know. I do, too, but we both know what would happen. Patrick would brutalize Heath and then wind up in prison for the rest of his life. He wouldn't stand a chance against the Seatons."

"He'd do it anyway," Bix said. "Knowing that, he'd still do it."

"I know. I love him for that, but I wouldn't let him do it."

Bix held Colleen's face in her hands. "And that's why you and I are friends, because you wouldn't let Patrick go down that hole. I've known Pat a long, long time. He deserves someone like you who cares about him." She patted Colleen's cheek. "So let's fix this mirror so that he never finds out what happened."

"How are we going to do that? I have no idea how to reattach a mirror."

Bix laughed. "Shit, honey, do you know how many mirrors I've glued back on to the pieces-of-shit cars I've driven my whole life? I've glued on mirrors and tied on bumpers and taped down trunks and hoods. Hell, I even caulked a wrong-size windshield onto this car I stole in high school. A little mirror like this? Nothing to it. We just have to find some epoxy."

"Oh." Colleen followed Bix to a maze of shelves. "Where would it be?"

"Anywhere." Bix waved over the racks of boxes, tools, and canisters. "Just look around."

"What does it look like?"

"Like epoxy." Bix huffed. "Like a tube of glue. Trust me. I know there's some around here. We used to buy it by the case when we were just starting out. That and chicken wire were the only things that held our old trucks together. I'd bet my teeth that John has knocked off more than one mirror on those new trucks they've got. He drives like a maniac when he's sober, though he's not sober much."

While Bix searched through the bins on a wall of shelves, Colleen pretended to search along the low racks that lined the outer wall of the office. She had no idea what she was looking for. She found metal bits and rolls of wires, small plastic bundles that looked something like fuses. There were boxes of filters and bottles of solvents and oils with numbers for names.

"What is all this stuff?" she asked, ducking around a curtain of tarps draped over a pipe rack. "How do you find anything?"

"There's an order to it," Bix said from somewhere within a fortress of pallets. "The layout was my idea. Patrick wanted everything set out in straight lines and orderly stacks."

"What's wrong with that?" Colleen asked, opening a closet that jutted out of the wall past the office door.

Bix clucked her tongue. "Lord, you and Pat are a tidy pair, aren't you? But tidy doesn't mean shit when it comes to business. A potential client comes in to your business and sees that it's all tidy and neat, what's he going to think?"

Colleen peeked around the mostly empty closet. "That it's a business run by adults?"

It seemed strange to her that, in the middle of the jumble of equipment strewn about the hangar floor, a little storage room like this would
stand nearly empty. It was too narrow to have ever been an office—six
feet wide at best but twice as deep lined on both sides with heavy-duty
shelves bolted to the walls. It was open at the top, lit only by the overhead lights of the hangar. Colleen would have thought it a perfect place
to store whatever all that stuff was they'd been poking through. Instead,
these shelves were nearly bare except for a few bottles of motor oil, a
couple of cartons of paper, and some other odds and ends. Nothing
that looked like epoxy.

"No," Bix said. "He's going to think you're a prissy fucker who's
more worried about being anal than getting the job done. He's also
going to think that nobody hires you since you have so much time to
fuss around with—oh, here it is!"

Colleen stepped out of the closet to see Bix heading for the car,
holding a small box.

"Looks like they just got a couple new boxes of it, which means
John's probably been driving again." She snorted at her own joke. She
tossed Colleen the black box that was no bigger than a carton of toothpaste. "Read the instructions to see how long it has to cure. I'll go find
us some rags and duct tape to hold it in place."

"There are rags in the closet," Colleen said, squinting to read the
finely printed directions on the little box. She heard Bix talking to
herself as she found rags and tape and started fiddling with the mirror.

"Yeah," Bix said, holding the mirror in place. "This broke off clean.
We won't have any trouble at all fitting this back on. It'll hold a good
seal. You'll have to get the wires reconnected if you want to use the
controls but you can do that later when you're not freaked out. How
long does the box say we have to hold it?" She put the mirror down and
pulled a cigarette out of the pack in her shirt pocket.

"It says this stuff is incredibly flammable. Don't light that cigarette."

Bix laughed. "Hell, it always says that stuff is flammable. Everything is flammable. Even water if you dump enough shit in it. Just read the part about the hold."

Colleen kept reading. "No, it looks like this stuff is super flammable. Like explosive. Are you sure this is safe?" When Bix huffed in frustration, Colleen held out the box. "Look at it. All of this writing? Warnings about flammability. The directions are just one line. The rest is guaranteeing us we're going to die a fiery death."

Colleen read aloud from a box of bold print. "'Danger. Extremely flammable liquid and vapor. Vapors may cause flash fire.' And here: 'Contains solvents that outgas while curing.' What does that even mean? I don't know if we should use this. I don't want to burn the hangar down."

"Oh for fuck's sake, Colleen, it's glue. What do you think it's going to say? Do you know how many times we used to get high sniffing this stuff?" She grabbed the box and pulled out the tube. "Don't be such a chicken shit. Here's the directions." Colleen noted that Bix's fingertip was more than halfway down the text littering the tube. All the other dense type was listing the incredible dangers of the product within.

Bix wiped down the rubber gasket where the mirror had been as well as the inside of the mirror connector. "See? None of this is broken off. We just need to make sure that there will be a solid connection." She opened the tube and squirted out a thin line of epoxy on the gasket and the mirror. The liquid oozed out like a shiny black worm. Thin spiderwebs trailed off where Bix scraped the tube to cut off the glue. She capped the tube and slipped it back into the box.

"We just let these get tacky. Shouldn't take but a few seconds and then we put them together." With a steady hand, she slid the mirror into place over the gasket, wiggling it just a bit to be sure of the fit. Holding it with one hand, she grabbed a rag and wiped up the tiny fibers of trailing glue.

After a minute, she looked back at Colleen. "Now pull me a couple of long strips of duct tape. It's right there by the closet." Colleen grabbed it and pulled a length of tape out but didn't tear it off.

"How long?" She held it out for Bix to see. "Is this long enough?"

"Longer," Bix said. "We need it to run from the windshield over the mirror and to the door. Pull two or three of them. Longer is better than short." Colleen did as instructed, feeling stupid needing instructions even for something as simple as pulling tape. Bix put piece after piece in place, securing the mirror. When she was done, she stood up and wiped her hands on her jeans. The car looked like a junker, the ugly gray tape streaming across the side of it, but the mirror stayed in place.

"Perfect," Bix said, smiling at the work. "The tape is probably overkill. That epoxy could glue a man to the ceiling but I'd rather be sure and I don't feel like standing here all day holding the mirror in place." She turned to Colleen. "What do you think?"

Colleen smiled. "Wow, I'm impressed that you knew how to do that. I never would have figured that out. Are you sure it's not going to catch on fire?"

Bix laughed out loud. "You are such a girl, Colleen." She waved her hands over her head, feigning panic. "'Oh my lord! Oh my lord! I'm on fire! I'm burning! I'm melting! Help!'"

"Shut up," Colleen laughed. "That box made it sound like a nuclear warhead."

"This box"—Bix picked up the glue—"was written by lawyers who want to cover their asses. If you start paying attention to all the warning labels in the world, you'll be too scared to leave your house. And speaking of leaving the house, now that you're out, why don't you come to my place? You look like you could use a drink."

Colleen hesitated. Patrick would be home this evening. They needed to talk. That meant Colleen needed a clear head. But Bix had really come through for her. And she really could use a drink. Bix sealed the deal with her next observation.

"That glue has to dry for a while. I wouldn't risk driving it until we're sure the bond is set. Why don't we leave your car here, go to my house for a cocktail, and you can tell me everything that happened today and I can tell you more about the shit-show that is my husband. Then when the glue seal is nice and tight and we're good and loose, I'll drive you back here to get your car. Sound good?"

Colleen grinned. "That sounds like a plan."

Bix winked. "Let's hide this tube so they don't know we did this." She ducked into the closet Colleen had been searching. Bix tossed the epoxy out of sight behind the cartons of paper on the top shelf. "We'll get it when we come back for your car. Your secret will be safe forever! Unless we get too drunk and blab it out. It's a fifty-fifty shot."

"I'll take those odds."

· · · · · · · · · · · · · · · · · · · ·

After the day she'd had, Colleen felt relieved by Bix's need to talk about herself. Yes, she'd asked Colleen about the incident with Heath, but really, what was there to say? He'd terrorized her. Again. There seemed to be no reason for it except to prove to both of them that he could. There really wasn't anything she could do about it that wouldn't blow back badly on herself or Patrick, so there was no point in going over it again and again.

That worked out fine for Bix, who had plenty to say about John, starting with his drinking being out of control. Seeing as how Bix was halfway through her second gin and tonic before Colleen had put a dent in her first, Colleen understood Bix had to be talking about some serious consumption.

"I don't know if something has changed between him and Pat because you all got married or because of pressure from the business, but just this summer John went on a bender that, even for him, was epic. I know he was taking Lortabs and I was missing Xanax."

"You take Xanax? What for? If you don't mind my asking."

"For the hell of it. What do you think? It's a nice easy pill to take the edge off when liquor won't get you there." Bix lit a cigarette and fanned the smoke away. "Let me guess. You never take pills. You've never even smoked the devil's weed."

"I've gotten high before," Colleen said. "In high school and college."

"I bet." Bix smirked. "I bet you would smuggle out wine coolers under your plaid skirt and everyone would share a cigarette while you talked about French-kissing the boys from the military academy down the road. You giggled over what to wear to your winter formal."

Colleen rolled her eyes, trying to keep her impatience from sounding nasty. "Yeah, yeah, yeah. And while I was doing that, you were pulling off armored car heists and running heroin for the Mexican drug cartels." She felt the gin hitting the sweet spot. "Let me guess. You were sent to the big house for whacking a snitch. What did you do? Give him concrete shoes and throw him in the Hudson?"

Bix waited until she finished. "You've been watching too much *Sopranos*."

"Yeah, well that's what you all sound like when you start talking about it. It's like I married into *The Shawshank Redemption*, sometimes."

Yep, that gin was definitely setting in. Colleen realized with some pleasure that Bix didn't mind. She didn't have to be decorous around Bix. She didn't have to watch her mouth or measure her words. It felt good.

She might as well keep at it. "So what were you in juvy for? And don't start in about your nana in Williamsburg or whatever. Tell me the truth."

Bix barked out a laugh. "It was my mamaw in Williamson. Trust me, there's a big difference there."

"Whatever." Colleen took a deep sip. "Tell me the truth."

Bix picked up her gold Zippo lighter and started flicking it. Flip, light, flip, douse.

Colleen watched the flame appear and disappear over and over. "Is this supposed to mean something to me?"

Bix nodded. "This is what I did. I burned down my neighbor's shed. I didn't mean to. We were lighting zippers, aka white trash fireworks. You know what they are?" Colleen shook her head. "It's when you light a garbage bag on fire and throw it up in the air. It sort of burns and sparks and melts and it goes way up in the sky. Anyway, me and Buzzy Blankenship had broken into my neighbor's shed to find more plastic and I lit it too close to the shed. Burned the son of a bitch down."

"How old were you?"

"Eleven. They almost took me to juvy court then, but my mom convinced my neighbor that it was just an accident. He was just pissed because he'd been growing pot in that shed and we burned his plants and lights and stuff. I didn't know anything about pot plants at the time."

"So you didn't go? I thought you met John at juvy court?"

Bix laughed and put the lighter on the counter. "Aw hell no. I didn't go to juvy until I was sixteen. After that first time, I got a taste for it. I set fire to an old junker out in the holler. I started setting fires at school. I finally burned down the announcer's box at the little league field." She laughed at the memory. "That time I went too far for the law. I mean, shit, burn down the school? Alright. Damage the little league field? Alcatraz for you!"

Colleen watched Bix spin the lighter. "Why did you keep doing it?"

"Lord, if I had a dollar for every time someone asked me that question. Everybody was an expert. They said all kinds of shit—low IQ, sexual dysfunction, narcissistic tendencies." She shrugged. "I just liked it. I liked watching things burn. I liked the power, the way it scared everyone. I liked the way it damaged things in a way that couldn't be undone. Some damage can't be. I wanted to be the one who got to do that kind of damage." The lighter kept spinning even after Bix's fingers drifted away from it.

Colleen didn't know what to say to that. She knew there was more to that story, probably a lot more, and none of it would be easy to hear.

Bix stopped the lighter from spinning with a soft tap of her palm and looked up at Colleen. "We need another drink. You need another drink. I'm way ahead of you."

"I would never try to keep up with you."

"Nah, that would be dumb, but you can at least try to represent yourself." She laughed and fished out some fresh ice from the freezer. "I know I talk about what a wild kid I was and what kind of shit I came from. My mom was an old whore who never gave a shit about anything. But as bad as I had it, I'd go back for seconds and thirds before I'd spend half a day in Patrick's life. Has he told you any of his shit?"

Colleen watched Bix pour the gin. "Some. Not much. He doesn't like to talk about it and I don't like to pry. I've seen the scars. He's seen mine."

"I bet he's got a lot more than you do."

Colleen nodded. Patrick's body was riddled with old, deep cuts and burn marks. He had ridges where bones hadn't knit together properly. They read like a Braille code beneath her fingers, written in a language she couldn't understand, telling a story he didn't want to relive.

Bix shook her head. "Me and John were just, you know, the usuals. John's parents were drunks. Kind of harmless but the kind that catch the social workers' attention, you know what I mean? He'd come to school dirty. They were always getting their power and water turned off. The kids would wander off while their parents went on binges. But they seemed like kind of a nice family. I mean, they were shit for parents, but John still loves them.

"My family was one of those big, multigenerational train wrecks. Everyone living on the same property. Uncles and cousins coming and going, stealing shit and shooting at each other. Nobody watching to make sure the kids were okay. Nobody giving a shit if you were scared." Bix flicked at the lime wedge in her glass, sending it spinning. "But

Patrick? Man, Patrick was fucked from day one. And he was fucked for a good long time."

Colleen's stomach soured. She didn't know if she wanted to hear this.

"He came into Clark-Esler home the usual way. Teacher noticed some bruises, which was fucking hilarious because John told me that by that time, Patrick was always peeing blood. He was from out past Mud Creek in Pike County, way, way out in the hollers where there wasn't anything to do but drink Mountain Dew and get fucked up."

She lit a cigarette. Colleen noticed that for this story, her heavy accent faded. Her voice was soft and serious. "Problem was that his social worker had a taste for shit that his government salary didn't cover. This was back before Oxy had really hit and people were still grinding crank and crack. They'd get you good and fucked up, but they burned off fast. That meant you had to have a steady supply, and that got expensive."

Bix shaped her ash in the ashtray. "The only thing Pat's stepdad was better at than making crank was beating the fuck out of Pat. The only thing Pat's social worker wanted more than a steady paycheck was crank. You see where I'm going with this?"

Colleen didn't, but she knew with horrible certainty she would find out.

"They had a nice scam going. Pat would go into foster care. His social worker would do a 'home examination' and recommend that Pat be put back in his home for a trial period. Pat's stepdad got to keep getting the SSI for the kid but didn't have to feed him as often, and he still got the pleasure of regularly beating the shit out of him. And Milton Farrah, Pat's social worker, got a regular discount on his brain-melter."

"Oh my god."

"It gets better than that. Turns out that Milton Farrah bought his shit from more than one dealer and sometimes that dealer would accept alternatives to cash, if you know what I'm saying. Pat's home visits weren't always to his home."

"Oh my god." Colleen felt the floor falling out from beneath her.

"Yeah." Bix picked up her lighter once more. "For all the shit they talk about the Clark-Esler home, John said being there was the only safe place Patrick ever knew. That's why Green Fields is so important to him. That's also why he's such an insufferable prick about anyone taking drugs. He has the original zero-tolerance policy. And that's why he insists that any kids who want to be in special programs have to pass their drug tests."

"Oh my god." It was all she could say. She felt immediately and deeply stupid and indulgent and spoiled for all the times she had cried to Patrick about what she had suffered during her marriage to Heath. "How could that happen? How did nobody know about this?"

Bix blew smoke out her nose like a bull. "Honey, there is shit going on in this world you would never believe. You think anybody gives half a fuck about some fuzzy-headed little snot in Ass-Out Kentucky? Patrick was just one of a million kids like that—dirty, cheap, written off. He was listed as 'an anger problem' and 'prone to violence,' so even if he'd wanted to talk, nobody would have listened to him. And Milton Farrah, his social worker? He was just one of a million bottom-feeders who preyed on those kids. Nobody gave a shit about him either when he went missing."

"What happened to Milton Farrah?"

"Oh, you know." Bix sounded funny, looking at Colleen like they were sharing a secret. "Doing drugs never ends well for anyone. People get turned out, get wired up, get violent."

Colleen stared at her. "What are you saying?"

"I'm not saying anything." Bix held up her hands innocently. "I'm just saying that bad things happen to bad people and Patrick's anger problems landed him back at Clark-Esler for good when his social worker failed to report to work one day. Nobody else bothered to take up Pat's case and he got to stay until he graduated. That's when he and John got really close.

"It's a funny thing about John. From what I understand, Patrick was really hard to like as a kid but John stuck with him. They were tight. John is a lot of bad things but he is a really good friend." She laughed into her drink. "Of course, I played a big part in keeping both of them from screwing everything up. I can't imagine what a mess they'd have made of their company or Green Fields if I hadn't been there doing the hard work. I love both of those guys. I know you care about Patrick but you can't understand what it's like to come up like that, how it bonds you with the other people in there with you. John's a drunk, whoring son of a bitch but I love him. That's why I wish he'd tell me what is going on with Heath Seaton."

Colleen sighed and rested her chin in her hand. "Is he still in contact with him? I know you guys have seen some really horrible stuff. I may never sleep again after what you just told me about Patrick, but Heath Seaton is a monster of a different kind. He's not desperate and scraping by to make a living. He's evil. He's just evil because he's evil."

"Well, it sounds like he's also getting pissed." Bix pulled out the cloned phone. "I guess getting his ass kicked by Pat got Heath's dick in a twist because his messages have gotten a lot shittier. And they weren't that sweet beforehand. Like this one. *Fuck your cut-rate meat. You know what I want.* And this one. *One hour. One alibi or Amber Beth Cains gets famous.* Whoever the hell that is. He sent a bunch of names again, too—Angela Reeves, Luda Wayne Napier, Jefferson Lee Wallace. God, that's a boy's name. I guess they're dipping into that nastiness now."

"You've been getting these texts all weekend? Why didn't you tell me?" Colleen asked. "I could have told Alyssa about them. That might have helped figure out what's going on."

Bix snorted. "If I know John, he's going to fuck this up and it'll all just blow over."

"Trust me on this. Nothing just blows over with Heath."

Bix dropped the phone onto the counter. Colleen could see she was upset but didn't know if she should expect tears or anger. Bix sniffed. Tears it was.

"Maybe I didn't feel like parading my troubles around in front of your snooty friend."

Seriously? Colleen thought. This again?

Bix wiped her nose on the back of her hand. "It's just that it looks like John is going through with whatever his end of the deal is." She thumbed the phone to life and handed it to Colleen. The screen showed a text stream between John and another 606 number.

John: We had a deal. Can't control P.

606: Fuck your deal. New deal.

John: No names, no deal.

606: U know what I want. AND you get your dick wet or chop chop.

John: Get me the name.

"What the hell does any of this mean?" Colleen asked. "Get his dick wet or chop chop? What names? Do you have any idea what any of this means?"

"I know what it means to get your dick wet. It means—"

"I know what the phrase means, Bix. But what does it mean in this context? What is John buying? A hooker? Why does he need the name?"

"He hasn't bought shit." Bix snatched the phone away. "I check his personal accounts all the time, even the ones he thinks I don't know about. No money is missing."

"You check his accounts? How did you get his passwords?"

"I cloned his phone. You think his password was hard? John's a Duke fan. Look up March Madness, pick a score. Not tough." Bix lit a cigarette. "Don't you check Patrick's phone?"

"No."

Bix snorted. "Well aren't you precious? I guess if I was married to a tight-ass like Patrick I wouldn't worry either."

"Patrick is not a tight-ass." She put down Bix's phone. "And I don't check his phone because I trust him. And he lives up to that trust. Maybe if you and John would actually talk to each other instead of getting hammered all the time, you might—"

Another Bix-shift blew in, this time to anger. She jabbed her finger in Colleen's face. "Don't you tell me how to run my marriage." Her voice hissed out between her clenched teeth. Colleen could smell cigarettes and gin. "I don't need advice from you, okay? You got your ass handed to you by that nancy-boy Heath Seaton and now you've taken your purity vow with St. Patrick the Righteous. You have no idea what it's like to love a man like John Mulroney." Her finger kept jabbing. "He's a real man with real needs and real flaws who needs a real woman, not some white-bread, private school icebox. Don't you fucking judge me."

Colleen sat very still. "I'm not judging you."

"You're always judging me."

Colleen could hear Bix beginning to slur. Terrific, she thought, now Bix is going to get surly and I'm stuck here with no car. "I'd better call Patrick to see if he can come get me."

"I'll drive you."

"No, I'll just call Patrick."

"Oh fuck, Colleen, don't go running off with your tail between your legs just because I didn't kiss you on the mouth."

Colleen gathered up her purse and stood. "What does that even mean?"

Bix sighed, shifting to penitent. "It means I'm sorry I hollered at you. I'm sorry I turn into such a bitch sometimes. It's just that you get this wounded saint look on your face sometimes and it makes me feel like . . ."

"Like what?"

"Like you're caviar and I'm government cheese. I can't be like you, okay? I can't prance around in pearls and little sweaters, keeping my voice all low and soft, alright? If we're going to be friends, you've got to understand that this is the way I am. I'm not changing for you, for John, for anybody. This is me. This is who I am. And you know you want me for your friend because who did you call when you needed help? When your life got messy? You called me. Not your snotty golf club friends or your Keeneland Club ladies, you called me."

She held up that jabbing finger again but Colleen had stepped out of range. She poked the air with less vigor. "You never would have known how to fix your mirror. You'd have read those instructions and called the god damn fire department as soon as you opened that tube of glue."

Colleen could see that she had run out of whatever had been fueling her temper. Bix was right—she had come through for her when she needed help. She'd let her rant. She hadn't judged her for her anger or her frustration. Plus, she had known how to glue that mirror back on. Considering what would have happened had Patrick found out what actually happened, that was no small favor.

"Well, if it had been up to you," Colleen said, "you'd have just set my whole car on fire just to watch it burn. Firebug."

"Tight-ass," Bix said, trying to fight back a grin.

It seemed they were friends again.

CHAPTER FOURTEEN

Bix got Colleen home in one piece, in large part because traffic was slow on New Circle Road. The beltway around Lexington stayed slow until at least seven every weeknight. Colleen didn't mind the traffic. It kept Bix below the speed limit and her gin-fueled driving in check. Colleen had declined her offer to drive her back across town to the hangar to get her car. She'd had enough gin herself. It was best to get them both off the road. She hoped she wouldn't regret not calling Patrick.

"Holy shit," Bix hissed as she pulled up to Colleen's house. A Kentucky State Police car sat in the driveway where Patrick usually parked. "What do we do?"

"What do you mean, what do we do?" Colleen asked. "We ask what's going on."

Bix fidgeted in her seat. "Man, you have a much different reaction to the police than I do. Where I grew up, you see the cops, you run for cover. I guess that's different for a nice white girl like you."

"Uh, you're white, too."

"No," Bix corrected. "I'm white trash. That's a whole different race."

Colleen shook her head and opened the door. "Do you want to come in? Find out what's going on? Or should I pull out my tommy gun and lay down some cover fire so you can make your getaway, Ma Barker?"

"Joke all you want. The police don't show up to wish anyone a happy birthday." Bix waved her out of the car. "And if it's all the same to you, I'd rather not give them a chance to breathalyze me. I saved your ass once today. Now it's up to your husband."

"Whatever." Colleen climbed out of the car. The tension of her standoff with Heath had turned into stiff muscles in her neck and back. The gin had dulled her thinking but not her aches and her walk felt awkward. She just wanted to lie down and put this day behind her. She hoped the police were just there for a donation or something. She really hoped Patrick wasn't in the mood to have that long talk tonight.

The trooper sat in his car, writing on a clipboard. He looked up as Colleen approached and pointed toward the porch. She nodded and waited for him at the front door.

"Mrs. McElroy?" he said as he approached. "I'm sorry to bother you. Do you have a moment?" He adjusted his flat-brimmed hat and rolled his shoulders as if they'd gotten stiff from sitting.

"Yes. What's going on?" Colleen asked. "Is everything okay?"

The trooper hooked his thumbs in his belt. "Well, I was hoping to catch your husband at home. Figured I'd get a little paperwork done while I waited." He smiled down at her. "You don't know when he'll be home, do you?"

She shook her head. "He's working. He keeps long hours."

He nodded. "Don't we all. I'm awfully sorry to bother you, ma'am, but we have a girl gone AWOL from Green Fields."

"You're looking for her here?"

"We're hoping she might have gone somewhere familiar. I talked with Ginny Anderson out there at Green Fields—she's the one who made the call when the girl went missing—and she said that Luda Wayne was close with your husband, Mr. McElroy, and his partner, Mr. Mulroney. We're just trying to find her before she gets into any trouble."

"Luda Wayne?" she asked. "Luda Wayne Napier?"

"Yes, ma'am." He looked at her closely. "I believe she also goes by Ziggy."

Colleen didn't know what to say. Luda Wayne Napier was one of the names on the list that Heath sent John. She hadn't connected it to the angry girl who had enjoyed her scones at the hangar. "Have you asked John about her?"

"No, ma'am. The Mulroney house was my next stop."

"He's not there," Colleen said. "I was just there. Bix, his wife, just drove me home. John wasn't there."

The trooper nodded. "Well then, I guess we'll just have to keep an eye out. If Luda Wayne comes to you, Mrs. McElroy, I hope you'll encourage her to return to Green Fields."

"Of course," Colleen said.

The trooper thanked her and wished her good night. She watched his car back out of the driveway and disappear down the street. She stood there for a long moment, staring into the darkness before heading into the house.

CHAPTER FIFTEEN

Now what? Colleen stood in the hallway listening to the empty house.

Where was Patrick? Should she call him and tell him about Ziggy? About her name coming up in a text from Heath? What would he do?

What could she do? She couldn't even help look for Ziggy, since she hadn't picked up her car and she wouldn't have the first idea where to look for her. She was stranded with her questions and her anxieties. She considered calling Alyssa to tell her about the missing girl but she knew what her friend would say. There would be no rationalizations to put off calling the police. Colleen didn't want to accidentally involve her attorney in anything that could threaten her professionally.

She thought about calling Bix, but that thought died a quick death. Bix was John's wife. For better or worse, Colleen didn't doubt where her loyalties would lie. She would do whatever it took to keep her husband out of trouble, even if it meant endangering Ziggy. Bix and John and Patrick—thick as thieves, as the old saying went.

Colleen wondered if Ziggy had bonded with anyone after all her years in the system the way they had. Did she have a best friend or a cluster of kids like her who would come to her rescue? Is that what these group homes did, offer kids with broken families a new clan based on hardship?

If blood is thicker than water, what was this bond that was thicker than blood?

Whatever it was, she didn't share it with them.

Colleen clicked the light switch in the hall but nothing happened. Maybe a burned-out bulb. Maybe a short in the old wiring. Patrick would know. So would Bix, probably. All of them knew things like epoxy and wiring and freight scales. When they had cookouts, Colleen never went near the grill or fireplace. Patrick even put gas in her car and changed the oil in it, even though she never asked him to. She liked the thought behind the gesture, that Patrick was a man who took care of things.

She was less fond of the thought behind the gestures when it came to Bix and John. They often treated her like she was helpless and incapable. She thought about Bix laughing at her concern over the flammability warnings on the epoxy box.

Colleen headed down the dark hallway, trailing her fingers along the wainscoting. She wasn't helpless. She had felt capable and strong as a girl. Alyssa was right—Colleen had been outrageous and bold in her Mad Dog Dooley days at St. Agatha's. But those days were far away. Maybe she had just *felt* strong. While she'd been creating calligraphy scandals, Bix had been stealing cars and setting them on fire. Patrick had been enduring much worse.

God, what Patrick had endured. Colleen wandered into Patrick's office and lowered herself into his leather desk chair. She had gotten him this for his birthday. The soft leather cradled her, swallowing her. This chair fit Patrick. It engulfed her and she let it have her. It felt like Patrick—big and tough but soft and safe. Her feet barely touched the wheeled feet and she had to stretch her toe to push off and spin the chair in a lazy circle.

On the desk sat Patrick's iPad in its leather case. He kept his business records on it. Colleen flipped open the case and the screen came to life.

Password protected. A four-digit number needed.

She had never snooped on Patrick, not once, not even in the dizzy, breathless afterglow of their early days together, when he would climb out of her bed naked and sweaty from lovemaking. He would head to the shower or maybe to the kitchen. He loved to eat after sex and would always bring Colleen a glass of ice water to cool her down. He would leave his phone and his wallet and whatever else men carried with them in pants pockets and jackets, just leave them scattered where they had fallen, and she would play with the idea of poking through them—not looking for anything, just wanting to put her hands on more of him, to see him from every angle.

But she never did. His wallet remained a folded mystery, his driver's license and receipts and credit cards hidden from her, his phone just silent black glass. Sometimes she would touch them, tempting herself to open them, but then she would pull back her fingers and bring them to her face, to her lips, where his body had been.

The smell of him on her skin was better than any lifeless printed data or digital photo. The reality of his body was the only secret she wanted to uncover again and again.

Until now.

Now that number pad glowed in front of her. Bix had guessed John's password. She talked about it like a kid who has discovered where Mom and Dad hide the Christmas presents, like the secret she had unearthed was inevitably meant for her anyway, so why not help herself.

Colleen didn't pry. She didn't snoop. In her mind, privacy equaled dignity, personal possession. A human right.

Her fingertip smeared the glass where she traced the leather edge of the case.

John had secrets. Maybe terrible secrets.

Did Patrick?

Her fingernail picked at a little thread that frayed from the stitching. Just four numbers. What would they unlock? A malicious genie that would never be contained again? Or an acid that, once released, would seep and burn through the bonds of trust they'd built?

Could she even guess it? Had he chosen a random password or was it a significant series of numbers? What would it mean if he had chosen their anniversary for his password? If she typed in zero three zero two, March second, and it unlocked his screen, would that make her feel more loved, or more treacherous? Or both?

What if it didn't work? Would she feel hurt? Unimportant?

She punched in the number quickly before she could stop herself. Nothing. Then her birthday. Then his. Nothing.

She curled her fingers against her chest as if they had been burned. Stupid. She should never have tried this. How many passes did a person get to unlock an iPad before they got locked out? What if she locked up his tablet? He would know. He would know she had snooped.

But now the desire to unlock the tablet had become a need. She wiggled in the chair, feeling the urgency flash through her muscles. There was nothing on his iPad. There wasn't. She knew it.

No, she *believed* it. Now she had to know.

Colleen pushed back from the desk, unable to stay in his chair. What was wrong with her? She made herself leave the office, luring herself to the kitchen with the promise of another gin and tonic. Gin was better than snooping. A hangover was better than a broken marriage.

Patrick hated it when she drank too much. Patrick hated drugs. She'd learned the awful root of that bias today from Bix. Bix knew Patrick's past, knew his secrets and his ghosts. In some ways Bix knew Patrick better than she did.

"Damn it."

Colleen grabbed her phone from her purse. She needed to talk to someone. She needed to get out of her own head, to stop thinking so hard. Nobody made it easier to not concentrate than Bix and her endless chatter.

When she thumbed her phone to life, however, another thought occurred to her. Bix had guessed John's password. Some piece of stupid sports trivia—the four digits of a final score in some basketball game—that had meant the world to him. Patrick had always told Colleen that marrying her was the most important milestone in his life. Evidently that wasn't so. That date might be the happiest, but what was the most important?

Her thumb hovered over the Voice Search button. Could she just look up something like this? It worked in movies. Information just popped up neatly whenever anyone asked for it, but could she do it? Could Colleen unlock this mystery of her husband's password? Could she put the pieces together, find the information, solve the mystery, and unlock his secrets?

What was the most important date in Patrick's life?

Google's voice search let out its distinctive beep. All she had to do was ask. She tried to organize what she remembered from Bix's story.

"Social worker death, Pike County, Kentucky."

What was his name?

"Milton Farrah."

She watched the talk-to-text letters sort out the sounds, populating the screen with type. Another second and the screen filled with links. Social workers, Pike County statistics, deaths in the foster care system, an accident at a Kentucky fair.

Then an article from the *Herald-Dispatch*, June 24, 1992. "Social worker death ruled homicide. Drug use suspected. State police report Milton David Farrah of Inez was found bludgeoned to death on Rt. 23 . . ."

Her thumb hovered over the link. June 24, 1992. The date Patrick's slavery ended and his stay at the group home became permanent. She clutched the phone in her fingertips, taking exaggerated care not to open any links. She carried it that way back to Patrick's desk.

She didn't sit. It felt wrong to her, perverse even, to comfortably settle into Patrick's chair while she attempted this abominable break-in. *Abominable.* Not too strong a word for this. June twenty-fourth. Zero six two four. If that date unlocked the screen, what did that tell her? What did it say about her husband that this date held the key to his secrets? What did it say about her that she had drawn this conclusion?

It said that she believed her husband had murdered Milton Farrah.

He'd been a kid. Fifteen. From what Bix told her, they had been fifteen very hard years. Unspeakable. Beyond her ability to comprehend, she with her private schools and doting parents.

June 24, zero six two four. It might just mean the date was important to him, his liberation day, his D-day, Bastille Day, his Cinco de Mayo. Milton Farrah was found bludgeoned to death. It didn't mean Patrick had swung the weapon himself.

Her fingers moved quickly. Zero six two. She hesitated, then pressed four.

Nothing.

Breath she hadn't realized she'd been holding escaped in a rush and Colleen felt dizzy with relief. June 24 was just a date. It was not the key; it was just another date on the calendar. She went to clear her phone screen but read the headline again.

Milton David Farrah was found bludgeoned to death.

Found. On June 24.

Before she could think anymore, Colleen punched in four numbers.

Zero six two three. June 23.

The screen came to life.

CHAPTER SIXTEEN

Icons filled the screen, colorful little squares and symbols that Colleen couldn't focus on. A little chime went off and more squares appeared and all Colleen could do was stare. It had worked. What did that mean? What was she supposed to do with that information?

What do I do? What do I do? The words fluttered like panicked birds inside her skull, screeching and throwing feathers in a riot while an older voice, the voice of her mother and her grandmother and her headmistresses, shushed and calmed them.

Everything is fine. There is no need for hysteria. Be calm. Always be calm.

All she had done was unlock his computer. She had guessed the date. No point in jumping to conclusions if those conclusions were not immediately important. She straightened her spine, mindful of good posture. She tapped her pearls.

What mattered right now was not the password. It was not the ramifications of that date, nor her betrayal of his privacy. What mattered at this very moment was what Patrick might or might not have on his tablet. Did he know what John was up to? Was he covering for his friend? Or, god forbid, was he involved?

Order was preferable to panic, one step at a time far better than racing pell-mell off the cliff of conspiracy. She had opened the computer. Look at it.

There was the usual stuff—apps for calendars and contact lists, music and photographs. Colleen didn't know much about iPads but she could tell just by looking that many of these were just factory-loaded entertainment add-ons. Did Patrick have a game log-in? Funny, Colleen couldn't imagine her serious husband ever managing a Sims town or shattering jewels on a timer.

Her success in locating the information on Google strengthened her resolve in the face of pages and pages of innocuous-looking icons. Folders, many of them labeled "MB." Macaroni Brothers. Finance, Receipts, Lading, Permits, Contacts, Insurance, Taxes, Schedule, Equipment, Rental. She clicked open a few folders—grids of document icons with dates and codes and names she didn't recognize, but nothing that looked out of place.

What was she hoping to find? A folder labeled Nefarious Deeds?

Finance seemed the most promising, what with money being the root of all evil. But if there were anything hidden in those documents, it would take someone far savvier than Colleen to figure it out. Rental estimates, payroll estimates, tax estimates, budget predictions—a flood of icons. How did Patrick keep all of this straight?

Scanning through Receipts and Lading and Permits just deepened her awe. Even a small business like Macaroni Brothers apparently required a library's worth of paperwork to function. How did Patrick manage all of this? Bix said John never helped but surely this was too much work for one man. No wonder he relied so much on Bix.

She scanned more quickly as she opened and closed files. Permits, Contacts, Insurance—they got denser and more boring as she read. She had her finger on the icon to close Insurance and move on to Schedule when she spied a folder within a folder.

Under Insurance, within MB Equip, was a document labeled AHG. The name stood out for its brevity—no dates, no numbers, shorter than all the other document names. It sounded like an insurance company or one of the equipment suppliers, but something about it caught Colleen's eye.

AHG. Arlen Henderschott, Gables? Could be. Could be American Hardware and Glass. Or All Happy Goats or Atlanta's Horniest Girls. There was only one way to find out. At the tap, the screen filled with an Excel sheet. A ledger.

It didn't supply much information. A category was labeled "A-." Six names appeared underneath the heading. Beside the names, a series of columns stretched out labeled with alphanumeric codes that meant nothing to Colleen. Most of the columns were empty except for maybe a dozen check marks scattered among the names. Only one column had no gaps, the column labeled DCBS. Each cell beneath that heading had a number.

The Department for Community Based Services. Foster care.

Colleen glanced at the footer of the file. It wasn't long, only seven pages. It held little information that she could decipher. Just names and DCBS numbers and a few checkmarks in boxes that meant nothing.

What was this? Colleen sat on the edge of Patrick's chair, her hands hovering over the sides of the tablet as if it might explode. So her husband had a ledger with names of foster kids. No mention of their ages, but if what Alyssa had found out was accurate, many of these names were no longer in foster care. They had aged out or graduated or whatever it was that happened to kids the state didn't worry about anymore.

She flicked to the second page. This group was labeled "A+." Probably a glitch in the database system, listing them alphabetically rather than by grade. She wondered if that irritated Patrick and his sense of order. It seemed the kind of thing that would irk him, like finding spilled salt on the counter where he set down a glass.

Only four names on this page. Not many more check marks in the columns. As curiosity began to outweigh fear, Colleen looked more closely at the names. First on the list of A+ was an Amber Beth Cains. That was the name Heath threatened to make famous. Beneath her name, in the same Excel cell, was a phone number.

She didn't give herself time to doubt or question. Colleen opened her phone and typed in the number. The area code was 304. Where was that? What would she say to whoever answered? No time to worry about that, either. Colleen hit the call button.

A woman answered on the second ring. "Hello?" Her voice sounded young.

Colleen pushed back from the desk, nearly dropping the phone. No, she could do this. Adopting the tone she had heard so often from the reunion committee of St. Agatha's, Colleen smiled as she spoke. "Hello, may I speak with Amber Beth Cains, please?"

"This is her. This is she."

Colleen could hear the nervousness in her self-correction. Trying to make a good impression. Who was she expecting to call? "Hi, Amber, I'm calling for Patrick McElroy."

"Oh hi!" The pleasure in her tone took Colleen by surprise. She didn't say anything for a moment and Amber rushed to fill the silence. "I appreciate you calling. I really apologize that I haven't stayed in touch. I've been meaning to send you all an update and to let you all know how everything turned out. And a thank-you card."

A thank-you card?

"Oh good," Colleen said. "Can you tell me more?"

"Yeah, oh yeah, everything turned out great. Like you all said, no problems at all." The more she talked, the younger Amber sounded. "I got the job at the rec center and I'll be starting junior college in the spring. I had to wait for the next semester to apply because there was a screwup with my application."

Amber's girlish voice chattered on brightly about her plans to be an X-ray technician and her new apartment and the terrific deal she got on a Ford Fusion. Colleen listened, inserting pleased hums in the proper moments to keep the girl talking.

The girl sighed and Colleen could hear a wet sniff through the phone. Tears.

"I just want to tell Mr. McElroy that whatever he wrote in my recommendation really made a difference. I really appreciate it and I really appreciate the opportunity I've been given. They were right; it was all worth it. I know you all have probably heard this a hundred times, but I'm clean and I'm staying clean. I got a second chance—heck, I've had a lot more than two, but this one I'm not blowing." Another sniff and then the sound of a nose being blown.

"I promise I'll send a Christmas card with my new address." She sniffed and laughed at the same time. It came out like a hiccup. "There's just one thing, though. You have to tell Mr. Mulroney something. Tell him that the good news is I'm not a UK fan anymore. The bad news is I'm still not a Duke fan. I'm in Huntington now. I'm a Marshall fan. Go Herd!"

Colleen laughed along with her, pretending she understood any of this. "I'll be sure to tell Patrick how well you're doing. I know he'll be pleased."

"Thanks. Thank you so much." Amber's voice got thick with tears once more. "I know it was a big risk. I mean, it was physically a risk for me, but you all took a big risk, too. I really appreciate that. I don't have any family, you know. Well, you all know. It means a lot to me that you all still check up on me."

Colleen put her hand to her forehead. What the hell had she expected? "We only want the best for you, Amber." She went to close the file, feeling stupid and embarrassed by her paranoia. A list of names of kids from foster care. Probably all kids with drug problems, a personal crusade for Patrick. He hated drugs but he loved these kids.

As Amber continued chattering on, Colleen flipped back and forth through the ledger. So many people. There had to be forty names on this list. On the fifth page, she noticed the header change. After "A-," "A+," "B-," "B+," she expected to see "C-." Instead she saw "AB-."

"Amber?" She cut the girl off midsentence. "What's your blood type?"

"It's A positive." Then she laughed. "You guys are still on top of it, aren't you?"

"What?" Colleen felt something cold awaken in her gut.

"Still keeping on top of the medical records? That's kind of what inspired me to get into hospital work. I mean, I went to a lot of group homes but I never had as many medical tests in my life as I did at Green Fields."

CHAPTER SEVENTEEN

Colleen sat silently, her phone dark in her lap, the iPad gone back to sleep. She'd gotten off the phone with Amber Beth Cains with some simple niceties and praise and the promise to relay all of her good news to Patrick and John. By her own admission, Amber had gone from a troubled, drug-abusing teen to a productive, healthy, and optimistic young woman thanks to the assistance of the Macaroni Brothers, Green Fields, and the Gables Medical Center.

That hardly seemed villainous. How could Amber Beth Cains be a threat to John? Why did Patrick have this list, but not John, if it dealt with foster kids? Had Patrick mistrusted John so much that he had distanced his business partner from the good work they had set out to do?

She closed the case of the dark tablet. She could forgive herself the intrusion into Patrick's personal belongings. He would never have to know because there was nothing she needed to confront him about.

She heard the jingle of Patrick's keys at the front door.

· · · · · · · · · · · · · · · · · · · ·

She hadn't wanted to talk tonight. She was tired and the gin rolled through her empty stomach, but none of that mattered now. She had to talk to Patrick about this. The list, the encounter with Heath, and now Ziggy missing from Green Fields. Her thoughts whirled as she tried to figure out where to start. She met him in the kitchen.

He squinted at her. "Are you drunk?"

"No." Her cheeks grew hot. "I had a drink with Bix. I had a bad day."

He shook his head and stepped past her, headed down the hall for his office. "I hope you can find better ways to deal with bad days than getting drunk with Bix."

"Where are you going? We need to talk."

"I've got work to do, Colleen."

"Are you working with John?"

Patrick snorted. "Work is not really John's thing."

"Ziggy is missing," she said. "Is that John's thing?"

Patrick moved slowly back into the kitchen, watching her. "What are you talking about?"

"Ziggy's real name is Luda Wayne Napier. It was on a list that John had on his phone." She watched Patrick's face for some reaction but he had turned to stone. "Her name was just one on a long list of girls. Now she's missing."

"What do you know about this list? Where did John get it?"

"Are you asking me that because you don't know?" Colleen met his stare. "Or because you want to see how much I know?"

"What are you talking about?"

"I'm talking about John Mulroney, your best friend and business partner, passing around lists of names of girls with Heath Seaton." Her voice rose. "I'm talking about you and John fighting more than ever, John drinking even more than usual. I'm talking about you *not* talking about the fact that we both know he's been hanging out with Heath."

He glared at her, still not moving, still not speaking.

Colleen folded her arms and leaned against the kitchen counter. "So I guess what I'm talking about is what we need to talk about. I need you to look me in the eyes and tell me that you are not covering for John Mulroney. That he has not gotten into some kind of mess that he expects you to bail him out of."

Still Patrick said nothing and Colleen shook her head in disbelief. "Okay, Patrick. You don't want to talk about this. You and John have your bromance, blood-brother, foster-care oath of solidarity. I get it. But you should know this. John is in regular contact with Heath Seaton and Heath almost killed me today."

"What?" His voice was a whisper.

"Oh, that gets your attention? Why does that surprise you? You know he tried to kill me when we were married. John seems plenty comfortable putting that in the past. But today, Heath followed me after I met with Alyssa. He ran me off the road out past Faulkner Avenue. He did it on purpose and he did it to scare me. And it worked. I was terrified."

"Are you okay?"

"You want to make sure I'm okay? Then tell me the truth. Tell me what is going on with you and John and Heath Seaton. What is this list they're passing around? Why was Ziggy's name on it?"

Patrick scrubbed his face with his hands. Colleen crossed to him and grabbed his hands in her own. She leaned in close.

"Listen to me. I know how convincing Heath Seaton can be. He's got a lot of money and he has a lot of contacts. He knows you all are hungry to grow. But believe me when I tell you that he *hates* me. He got off on hurting me when we were married, and now that I've taken all that money from him in the divorce, he hates me even more. And I know how well Heath can hate." She squeezed Patrick's hands.

"And because I love you, Patrick, you can believe that Heath hates you, too. No matter what he might tell John, he will do anything to hurt you. So whatever he has promised you or John, he is—"

Patrick's phone buzzed. He turned from her and checked the screen. "Colleen," he said without looking up from it, "I don't have time to explain this. I have to—"

"Oh my god." She spun from him, shaking her head. "Of course you don't have time. You have to go run an errand for Arlen Henderschott, don't you? You have to go fetch for your new business partner, your new lord and master."

"Colleen . . ."

"Of course! Why didn't I see it? You and John and Heath and Arlen, such a tidy foursome. Such a brilliant arrangement!"

"You don't understand."

"Sure I do!" She laughed. "Well, as much as a rich daddy's girl like me can understand such a thing. When I met you, you and John were hustling to scrape by. You were working yourselves to death trying to build the business." She cocked her head. "Whose idea was it to sign a deal with the devil, Patrick? John's? Yours? Who first decided to sell his soul to Arlen Henderschott and his imp brother-in-law, Heath? Exactly how much money did you get for your soul?"

Patrick's face was dark. "You have no idea how much pressure I'm under."

"Then explain it to me."

"I am not in a position to say no to Arlen Henderschott."

There it was, the truth Colleen feared. She could see it all over his face. "John got you in trouble. John got you into debt with Arlen."

Patrick clenched his teeth, making the muscles in his jaws twitch. Colleen could see the effort he put into controlling his temper. "John made a mistake two years ago. Before you and I met. He did something really stupid that would have gotten us into a lot of trouble."

"Tell me."

"I can't."

"You can." She forced herself to relax, to take the confrontation out of her voice. "You can, Patrick. I'm your wife. Tell me."

"He got a girl pregnant."

Colleen waited for more but Patrick just stared at the floor. "And? This isn't the fifties. And Bix isn't exactly a naïve bride. Surely there was a solution that didn't involve—"

"She was fifteen. She was at Green Fields."

"Oh." Her mouth went dry. "Oh."

"Yeah." Patrick's voice was soft. "I don't know how Arlen found out. I don't know if she went to him or he somehow found out from the Health Department. I don't know. All I know is that she was causing a scene. She wanted money. She was going to tell the police."

"She was fifteen."

His tone turned to ice. "She was a hard fifteen."

"She was fifteen! John was an adult. You can't be defending him!"

"He is my best friend and my business partner."

"And he's a predator!"

"Colleen." Patrick stepped forward and grabbed her by the upper arms. She could feel the strength in his hands. She knew what he was holding back. "You didn't know her. She had been turning tricks for years. She wanted money and she knew that if she filed sexual assault charges, that would be the end of Green Fields. She knew how much that meant to me and to John. She knew that if he got labeled a predator, we would never be able to work with those kids again. She knew she had us where she wanted us."

Colleen stared up at him. "Maybe you shouldn't work with those kids. If they're not safe with you, if John is a danger to them—"

"He's not." His fingers tightened on her arms, not enough to hurt, but close. "He's stupid and he did a stupid thing and Arlen helped us take care of it. He got her an abortion. He gave her money. He made her go away."

"Oh, well then," Colleen said, smirking, "everything worked out just fine. John ruins a girl's life, Arlen covers it up, and you two are in his pocket for the rest of your lives."

"Her life wasn't ruined. I swear it. She got a lot of money."

Colleen laughed an ugly laugh. "Ah yes, money. That fixes it."

"You don't understand."

"Right. Right. I don't understand because I'm rich. I was born rich and I got richer when I married into Arlen's family. Well, technically I got richer when I *survived* marrying into his family, but why split hairs? I got the money and that's what counts."

Patrick let go of her arms. He wouldn't look her in the eye.

"So what happens now?" she asked. "What is this new venture? Is Ziggy trying to ruin John's life, too? Is that what happened to her? Did she run away after trapping John with her incredibly powerful fifteen-year-old sexual wiles?" Patrick turned away from her but she followed, stepped in front of him, refusing to be ignored. "And are you just going to cover it up again? Are you going to let the Henderschotts and the Seatons buy off another girl? Or has John stepped up the business? Is that what the list is? Did Heath maybe convince John to take it to the next level? Pay the girls up front?"

"Colleen." He pushed away, turning his back to her. "Stop it."

"No, Patrick. I won't stop it. I don't owe John whatever it is you owe him. My loyalty doesn't go that far." She stared at his back. "Do you know where Ziggy is?"

"No."

"I don't believe you."

He turned to her. "I don't know where she is."

"Did John take her?"

"I don't know."

Colleen didn't have to hear any more. She believed what Patrick said and she understood what he didn't say. He didn't know if John had taken Ziggy.

But they both feared he had.

CHAPTER EIGHTEEN

Colleen jumped at the ringing of her phone. Patrick crossed his arms, scowling, while she pulled it from her purse.

"It's John." She held the phone up to show him, as if he wouldn't believe her.

Patrick's eyes widened and he nodded for her to answer.

"Hey, Colleen!" John's voice was bright and loud, as if they cheerfully chatted on the phone all the time. He spoke quickly. "Hey, uh, don't let Pat know it's me, okay? Okay? Is Pat there?"

Patrick could clearly hear his partner's voice because he shook his head and put his finger to his lips for silence.

"Uh, no. Patrick's not here. He had a meeting with a client." She scrambled to think of a convincing lie. "In Bowling Green." Patrick nodded his approval.

John's laugh sounded shaky, with none of its usual easygoing charm. "Oh, that's Pat, huh? Always working. Hey, um, I need your help. Can you do me a favor? A big favor?"

Patrick nodded again so Colleen answered. "Sure. What's up?"

John breathed hard into the phone and Colleen could make out some sounds of movement in the background, as if someone were bumping into the phone as he held it.

"Hey, Colleen, do you think you could come to the hangar? Ziggy is here. You remember Ziggy, right?"

Patrick's eyes widened in disbelief and Colleen held up her hand to keep him quiet.

"Yeah, I remember Ziggy. The police were just here looking for her. They said she ran away from Green Fields. Is she okay?"

John made a sound that might have been a laugh. "She's here. She's upset, you know? You think you could come out and talk to her? Just you? She likes you."

"Maybe we should call Green Fields."

"No, no, no!" John wasn't doing a very good job of not sounding panicked. "Don't do that. Don't do that, okay? It's just, you know, she's a little fucked up, you know? She took something and if they find out, she'll have to go back to court, go to juvy. You know, it'll be a whole big thing." He was speaking so quickly she could barely make out the words. "So will you come, Colleen?"

She looked to Patrick, who scowled and then nodded.

"Okay," she said. "I'm on my way."

"Oh, and hey, Colleen? Colleen?" John was nearly shouting. "Don't tell anybody you're coming, okay? Just come by yourself, okay?" He tried to offset the oddness of the request with a shaky laugh. "I mean, you know how Bix is—drama, drama, drama. And Pat can be a real prick when it comes to these kids doing any drugs. Ziggy really needs a break, you know?"

"Okay, John," Colleen said. "I'll be there right away."

"Great. Great. And Colleen?" He lowered his voice and sounded almost normal. "I appreciate this. I'm really sorry to ask you to do this."

The phone went dead.

· · · · · · · · · · · · · · · · · · · ·

Patrick stood with his back to her, his head bowed, his hands gripping the edges of the baker's rack like he planned to lift it over his head. Colleen could see the skin of his neck and jawline turning a deep red.

"Patrick? What do you want to do? Are you going to go with me?"

He didn't look up. "You're not going anywhere."

"But I told John I'd come out to help Ziggy."

Patrick shook his head, his hands flexing on either side of the cookbooks lined up on the rack. He was saying something but Colleen couldn't quite make out the words.

"Patrick? Talk to me."

"God damn it!" He spun, grabbing a small statue that had been holding up the books and hurling it against the far wall. "God damn it. God damn it. God damn it!"

Colleen couldn't breathe. She couldn't move. Patrick grabbed his hair with both of his hands, rocking back and forth. Colleen couldn't tell if he was trying to pull his hair out or keep his head on.

"Patrick, please. Talk to me. Do you know what's going on? Do you want to come with me to the hangar?"

His head snapped up. "I told you. You're not going to the hangar."

"But I said—"

"Colleen, have you not been paying attention? You're the one that told me that John is making deals with Heath. You said they were talking about making deals for girls, and now John has Ziggy at the hangar? Just like that? Nothing to worry about?" He stomped over to her and grabbed her by the shoulders. "That doesn't seem a little bit dangerous to you?"

She didn't know what to say. She wanted him to tell her what to do.

"I'm going to that hangar and I'm going to take care of this." He pulled her close and kissed her on the forehead. She could feel his hands twitching with anger. "You are going to stay here. Keep your door locked. Don't talk to John anymore. Don't talk to anyone, okay? You just stay here and let me take care of everything."

"What are you going to do? Shouldn't we call the police?"

His fingers tightened and then released. "I have to make a call first."

"Who? Who are you calling?"

He kissed her again and stepped away. As he turned back toward his office, he pulled his phone from his pocket.

"Patrick, who are you calling?"

"It's work," he said, walking away from her.

"Work? You're making a work call now?"

His only answer was the closing of his office door.

John had Ziggy. John was working with Heath. She leaned against the hallway wall. Would Patrick help Ziggy? Or would his loyalty to John win out over decency? How deep did this debt to Arlen go? Deep enough to make them both answer to Heath?

That punched feeling returned to her stomach and she had to bend over and put her head to her knees. She couldn't tell if she was hyperventilating or if she had stopped breathing altogether. Heath and Ziggy. Money and young girls. A list. A business. The possibilities fell onto her like a truckload of gravel.

No, not gravel. Shit. Vile, stinking filth.

Heath didn't buy prostitutes. He didn't spend his money on professional whores. That wasn't his thing. He liked to make clean women feel filthy.

It wasn't enough to hurt them. He liked to make them beg.

And then he liked to film it.

"Oh god." Colleen straightened back up. She turned to press her forehead against the wall. Slick sweat made her skin slide across the cool paint. She had to tell Patrick. If John and Heath were taking girls, she knew what Heath would do with them. Whether or not John was involved, whether or not he knew or would protest against it, if Heath Seaton had unbridled access to a vulnerable young woman, Colleen knew what he would do with her.

She thought of Ziggy, with those braids and that trying-to-be-tough smirk. She thought of her cautious enthusiasm at being emancipated. She thought of her stuffing her pockets with lemon scones. Oh god, if Heath Seaton had his way with a child like that, it didn't matter what Arlen might pay her afterward. She would never recover from it. There wasn't enough money in the world.

Colleen knew that for a fact.

She couldn't let Patrick cover for John. She couldn't risk his loyalty getting the better of him. It didn't matter how good a friend John had been. Heath Seaton was poison and, if she alone could see that, she had the responsibility to stop him.

. . . .

Patrick came out of the office and headed for the front door.

"Are you going to call the police?"

He stood for a moment with his back to her. When he turned, he looked calmer, more like the Patrick she loved. "No, Colleen. And please, don't you, either. I'm begging you, give me a chance to straighten this out. Please. I know it's a lot to ask, but let me try to fix this first. For John. For me. Please."

He waited, his hand on the knob.

She had a thousand things she needed to say, but she knew what his answer to all of them would be. He wouldn't turn his back on his friend.

She nodded. "For now."

"For now."

CHAPTER NINETEEN

Patrick hadn't been gone five minutes when the front door shook in its frame.

"Open the fucking door!" Bix pounded at the front door with what sounded like a battering ram. "If you're in there, you son of a bitch, I'm going to rip your fucking arms off and beat you to death with them! You worthless piece of shit! I swear to god."

Colleen rushed to get the front door open and get Bix inside before someone called the police. She had no more turned the lock than Bix barreled through, shouldering past her and running into the house.

"Where are you, you cheating motherfucker?" She slammed her fists against the doorframe of Patrick's office. "You'd better hide, because I'm going to kill you!"

"Bix!" Colleen shouted from the front of the hallway. "John isn't here."

Bix turned around, her face twisted in a junkyard-dog snarl. She marched toward Colleen, backing her up into the foyer, her long finger jabbing forward. "You tell me where he is, you lying fucking bitch. You tell me right now and don't give me any shit."

Colleen held her hands up. "Patrick is out looking for him. Right now. I swear."

"Fuck! Fuck, fuck, fuck!" Bix pulled at her own hair and slammed her shoulder against the wall. Colleen didn't know what to do. Bix had fifty pounds on her. If she decided to hurt herself—or Colleen, for that matter—there was little Colleen could do to stop her.

Bix finally stilled, her hands tangled in her hair, her forehead pressed to the wall, much the same way Colleen had been earlier in the evening.

"Bix?" Colleen kept her voice soft. She didn't need her to spin around with a haymaker and knock her teeth out. "Bix? Talk to me." She risked a soft hand on her shoulder.

"That son of a bitch." She breathed loudly against the wall, her nose pressed to the paint.

Bix was an ugly crier. When she started emitting a high whistling keening, Colleen almost wished she would get angry again.

"Come on," she said. "Come sit down. Tell me what's going on."

Bix allowed Colleen to lead her by the arm to the kitchen bar. That keening continued in rhythm with her breath, an awful *heef-heef-heef* sound that Colleen imagined one would hear in the corners of an insane asylum. The larger woman rocked on her stool, her feet hooked pigeon-toed around the lower rungs, her hands balled into fists in her lap. *Heef-heef-heef.*

Colleen had no idea what to do. Angry Bix had been scary enough. She had plenty of experience with funny Bix and drunk Bix and outrageous Bix, but freaked-out, shutting-down Bix? She had no playbook for this.

Bix pulled a pack of cigarettes out of her purse, shook one out and stuck it in her mouth. As she fished her lighter from her pocket, she saw Colleen's look of disapproval.

"I am smoking this fucking cigarette. Jesus, Colleen, could you maybe not be a tight-ass right now? I just lost my husband tonight."

The threat of those tears carried more weight than her argument, so Colleen put a little water on a saucer to use as an ashtray. Bix blew out a long stream of smoke, sighing and making a show of it. "Thank you." She flicked her lighter open and closed, open and closed.

"You're welcome. Now you've got your cigarette." She scowled at the smelly smoke. "Talk to me."

Bix took another deep drag and jabbed the cigarette toward Colleen. "Maybe you ought to be the one talking, huh? Since you and John are so tight."

"What are you talking about?"

Bix blew smoke out her nose like a dragon. "Aren't you a cool one? Butter wouldn't melt in your mouth, would it, princess?" She slammed the cloned phone down onto the counter. "This ring any bells for you?"

Of course. With the cloned phone, Bix would know that John had called her.

"You tell me what I ought to think," Bix said. "And don't you fucking lie. What did he say to you, Colleen?"

Colleen kept her voice calm and low. "John did call me. He wanted me to meet him at the hangar tonight. He sounded very strange."

Bix stared hard at her. "You didn't go?"

Colleen held up her hands. "Obviously not."

Bix stubbed the cigarette out on the kitchen counter. "Get in the fucking car. We're going to that hangar."

. . . .

Bix roared out of Colleen's neighborhood. The worst of rush hour traffic had subsided and Bix made good time on New Circle Road. She jammed a cigarette into her mouth and lit it with her gold lighter. She punched the button to crack her window, letting in a cold burst of rain and wind. Even in the dim lights of the dash, Colleen could see the anger burning on her face.

"I'm going to kill him. I don't care what his excuse is, what kind of bullshit he's got to say about this, I'm going to kill him."

She kept flicking the lighter open and closed, open and closed, until finally Colleen snatched the lighter away and stuffed it into her own pocket and said, "Keep your hands on the wheel and listen to me. We don't need to go to the hangar. Patrick is on his way there. He told me to stay put, to stay away from the hangar. If Heath is there—"

"Fuck Patrick. Fuck Heath. And fuck that fucking hangar." Bix slammed her hands against the steering wheel. "John thinks he's getting a fucking playmate tonight? He's in for a great big surprise."

Colleen held her purse in her lap. She considered sneaking her cell phone out and calling Patrick to warn him that Bix was on the warpath. She hoped she could somehow slow her friend down, talk her out of whatever vengeance she had planned for John, at least until Patrick had a chance to figure out what was really going on.

"I think our focus ought to be on Ziggy," Colleen said.

"What the fuck does Ziggy have to do with this?" Bix snapped.

Colleen told her about the state trooper stopping by with news about Luda Wayne Napier. "Didn't you recognize that name when you saw it in John's texts?" Colleen asked. "It's kind of an unusual name."

"No," Bix said. "Why would I? Did you?"

"It's just that you always talk about how close you are to those kids, how involved you are in their lives. I thought you might have known their names."

Bix waved the cigarette close to Colleen's face. "Don't you start with me. I don't keep all those little fuckers on my Christmas card list. I can't keep track of every little piece of trash that blows through those doors. And what's the big deal about Ziggy taking off? She probably ran off to sell her ass for pills."

"The big deal is that John called and said she was with him. At the hangar. He said she was fucked up and wanted me to come out and talk to her."

"You?" Bix laughed. "Why the fuck would she want to see you?"

"My question exactly. That's why Patrick went out instead. He said it sounded shady."

Bix took another deep drag and tossed the butt out the window. "That lying son of a bitch. That no good, lying son of a bitch, using that kid to get you there."

"What are you talking about?"

"You don't know?" She looked at Colleen. "You really don't know?"

"I don't know anything, Bix. I don't know why John called. I don't know why we're heading to the hangar. I don't know why you're so pissed off. I don't know anything."

"I'm pissed off because John is playing us both. That lying sack of shit. I'm pissed off because I've been reading his texts tonight. It seems like he's got all kinds of fun planned. Well let me tell you something, Colleen, I'm going to bust up that fun. I'm going to beat the shit out of his little playmate and then—"

"What are you talking about?"

"The text he got tonight!" Bix's voice was loud enough to make Colleen's ears ring. "It said *I got your playmate. Bring me mine.* And no sooner had that come through than John is on the phone to you. So you tell me what I'm supposed to be thinking, Colleen. You look me in the eye and tell me you're not planning on fucking my husband."

"I am not fucking your husband!"

As the words left her lips, Colleen realized what she had just heard. The pieces fell together with a sickening click, creating a picture she could not bear to look at.

A primal terror flashed through her body and it was all she could do to keep from throwing herself from the speeding vehicle.

"Stop the car. Stop the car, Bix." The words stuck in her throat. "We can't go. Turn around. Stop the car."

"The fuck is your problem?" Bix snarled.

"Playmate. Oh god. Playmate." Colleen put her head to her knees, curling into herself in the seat. That word. That was Heath's word. That was what he would call her when he was in the mood for something especially brutal.

"Bix, I'm not John's playmate. You've got this wrong. We've both got this all wrong."

"Snap out of it, Colleen. What do you have all wrong?"

Colleen squeezed her eyes shut. "Ziggy. Ziggy is John's playmate."

"What?" Bix laughed a harsh laugh. "Then who the fuck wants to play with you?"

Colleen couldn't speak the word.

CHAPTER TWENTY

Bix took the turn into the Medoc Industrial Park on two wheels. Colleen hung on to the dashboard, staring into the darkness of the asphalt and scrub grass stretching out in all directions. When they pulled up to the Macaroni Brothers hangar, two vehicles were parked at odd angles in the lot—a Macaroni Brothers van and Patrick's truck.

"It looks like one of the truck bay doors is open." Bix killed the headlights and pointed to the square of light spilling out on the concrete behind the building. "Let's go in that way. Quiet. Let's see what those sons of bitches are talking about."

Bix crept ahead of Colleen, holding her arm out to keep her behind her. At the open truck bay doors, she held up her fist like this was some sort of secret military operation. As ridiculous as it looked, Colleen had to admit she was glad Bix was taking point on this. The thought of the confrontation they might be walking in on soured her stomach and brought out a familiar anxious sweat along her hairline.

They heard arguing coming from within the hangar. Bix looked back at Colleen, put her finger to her lips, and together they slipped into the shadowed space. Straight ahead on the far wall of the hangar, the office door was dark. Someone had turned on a bank of lights over the racks of tools and equipment. To their right, the huge plane bay door was closed and locked, the Cessna shrouded in a tarp. In the center of the plane bay, Patrick and John stood facing each other.

There was no sign of Heath. Or Ziggy.

Bix squeezed Colleen's hand as they slipped in between the high shelves lined with boxes that separated the planes from the freight. Through a gap in the cartons, Colleen could see Patrick's profile. To see them, John would just have to turn his head a few inches, but he didn't. He kept his attention on Patrick.

That's when Colleen realized her husband had a gun.

She felt a surge of relief. It didn't look like John had a weapon. She could only get a clear view of him by risking a look through the shelves. Bix held her hand out, signaling her to stay back. Colleen watched Patrick through the gap. Bix watched with one eye around the corner of the shelf. Neither man had spoken since they had snuck in.

Patrick broke the silence. "Why are you doing this?" His voice sounded raw, almost sad.

"You know why."

"Please, John, don't do this."

"You're going to shoot me?"

"I don't want to." Patrick's voice cracked. "I just want the girl."

"I can't. Pat, c'mon."

Patrick raised the gun as John stepped closer to him. John lifted his hands. He didn't hold them up in surrender. He flopped them on top of his head, interlacing his fingers as he stared at his best friend. In that moment Colleen thought he looked a lot like her high school softball coach, who would take that same posture after one of his players had made an unbelievably dumb move.

John didn't look frightened. He looked shocked. He looked sad.

Patrick had tears in his eyes.

"Just walk away, John. I'll take care of everything. Give me Ziggy and walk away."

"Don't do this, man. Why are you doing this?"

"Why am I?" Patrick slapped tears off his cheek but kept the gun trained on John. "Why are you? I'm trying to fix this. I'm trying to solve this problem and you're fucking around with Heath Seaton. What did you think he was going to do? Help us? He is going to fuck us!"

"We are already fucked, Pat!" John yelled. "Don't you see that? I'm trying to get us out of this. I'm trying to fix this."

"Oh that's rich." Patrick's laugh sounded manic. "You're the fucking reason that list exists. You're the reason all of this is happening! You and your uncontrollable dick. If you had just—"

"Don't put this on me!" John stepped closer, ignoring the gun. "I paid my debt. We don't owe that piece of shit anything. Don't act like he's holding anything over on us. You saw that money and you got greedy. You wanted more."

"I got greedy?" Patrick's mouth hung open for a moment. "I don't remember you turning down any of the money when these deals started."

"I thought it was a scam! I thought we were running those guys, that we would just string them along. Just a bunch of rich assholes who think they can buy eternity. Fuck them, Patrick. That's what I thought we were doing." He shook his head and lowered his voice. "I never thought we were actually going to deliver."

Patrick brought both hands to his face, the gun pointing toward the ceiling. Colleen could hear his labored breath echo in the open space.

John stepped closer, his voice gentle. "C'mon, man, this isn't us. We don't do this."

Patrick jumped back when John touched his arm. He brought the gun down but kept it pointed away from John. "It's already in motion. The deal has been made."

"I made a new deal," John said. "You've just got to trust me."

"No. No." Patrick shook his head. "Arlen said if we pull this off, we get our cut and we're done. We're out. We just have to do this one time."

"And you believe that? It's never just once, Patrick. You know that! Didn't you learn that after that whole business with Amber? We kept digging that hole deeper and deeper and handing them the rope they're going to hang us with."

Colleen and Bix leaned against each other, watching their husbands. Colleen wondered if Bix knew any more than she did. What was "that business with Amber"? Amber Beth Cains? The happy young woman Colleen had spoken with on the phone today? Amber had mentioned a risk, but what had it cost Patrick and John?

John's voice had lost the shaky shrillness she'd heard on the phone. He sounded like the same easygoing fellow she'd known all along, and she could see Patrick relaxing as John spoke.

"Come on, man. You're right. I fucked up. I've fucked up a lot over the years, but this time I'm going to make it right, okay?" He gripped Patrick's shoulder. "Trust me this one time, okay? I can make this right."

"How?" Patrick asked.

"I got a plan."

Colleen heard Bix snort under her breath.

Patrick didn't seem convinced, either. "Tell me what it is." When John tried to dismiss the issue, Patrick shook him off. "No, John. I'm not trusting you on this. I want details."

"You don't need details, Pat, okay? The less you know, the better. Just trust me when I tell you that I'm doing this for you. For us. The Macaroni Brothers forever, right?"

Patrick looked as if he were on the verge of giving in when a slow clapping sounded from somewhere within the hangar. Bix and Colleen ducked down at the sound, uncertain where it came from within the cavernous space. It didn't take long to figure it out. All they had to do was look where Patrick pointed his gun.

Heath Seaton stepped out from behind the covered Cessna, clapping his hands slowly. The dim overhead lights shone off his pale hair.

"You two are adorable," he said, smiling to reveal small, white teeth. "Really, you are. Just like the Hardy Boys. I could listen to you two squabble all night, except that you're boring the shit out of me and I have better things to do."

Patrick kept the gun on Heath, but spoke to John. "You lying sack of shit. You looked me in the eyes tonight and swore to me that you weren't working with him anymore."

"Now, now, Patrick," Heath said, grinning. "To be fair, would you have agreed to his plan if you knew it involved me? How did you know it involved me, by the way?" When Patrick said nothing, Heath grinned again. "Doesn't matter. The fact is, John and I have a deal. You should be glad for it because it's going to benefit you in the long run."

Patrick looked to John but John only stared at the ground. "I'm listening."

"Are you, Patrick? Good. Because I've been looking forward to this for a while. In a way, I'm glad we had that little scuffle at Keeneland, because it upped my bargaining power with your partner."

"Is that right?" Patrick said, looking down on the smaller man who still bore the bruises from the beatdown. "Then what do you say we go for another little scuffle right now? See what kind of bargaining power you have when you're shitting your teeth out."

Heath pretended to shiver. "You're a hard man, Patrick. How hard do you suppose you're going to be in prison after I leak the files I took off Arlen's computer? My brother-in-law keeps excellent records of the people he's taking advantage of. He cooks his books so well that he comes out smelling like a rose while hard guys like you get dropped into deep, dark holes with no chance of parole." Heath winked at Patrick. "Those fighting skills of yours will come in real handy while you're fighting for the top bunk with Bubba."

"Hey now, come on, you guys," John stepped in, trying a little breathlessly to turn on the charm. "There's no reason it has to be like this. I know you guys don't like each other much and that's okay. That's what I'm here for. Patrick, Heath here can get us out from under Arlen's thumb. We don't have to do this job. We can just walk away and never look back. Isn't that right, Heath?"

Heath smirked at Patrick. "Sure is."

"What's in it for you?" Patrick asked.

"Oh, you'll find out soon enough."

John stepped between the two men, pushing Patrick back toward the plane bay door. "Come on, man. Trust me on this, okay? It's the only way." Patrick had let himself be pushed back a step or two when Heath spoke up again.

"Well, now, hang on a second." He spoke in that smooth cocktail party tone that Colleen remembered so well. He could make the vilest words sound like small talk. "Maybe Patrick ought to stick around. Maybe we should include him in our deal."

"No," John said, pushing hard against an unmoving Patrick. "We had a deal, Heath. You and me."

"Yeah we did and I held up my end of it. I've got that little girl tucked away somewhere real close, safe and sound. You can't find her without me. But as soon as I get what I want, you get what you want."

Colleen had become so mesmerized by the horror of her ex-husband's voice, she had almost forgotten that she and Bix were hiding. She felt as if she were sinking, drowning in the hard cement beneath her feet. Bix brought her back to reality by hissing in her ear. "Are they talking about Ziggy? What the fuck is so special about Ziggy?"

Whatever it was, it was keeping Patrick and John and Heath from killing each other.

Patrick let out a low laugh. "Man, you better get this show on the road because I'm thinking I'd rather blow your ass away and dump your body in the weeds than listen to any more of your shit." He aimed the gun at Heath. "I'm going to ask one more time. What do you want?"

Heath sighed and started to walk. He shook his head, ignoring Patrick and the gun. Instead he ambled along without a care in the world. As he came closer to the shelf behind which she and Bix were hiding, she could swear she smelled him. Bix squeezed her arm, urging her to keep still. That was unnecessary. Colleen had turned to stone. She couldn't have moved to save her life.

Heath proved that to be true.

"John? You want to tell him?" Heath trailed his fingers along the edge of the shelf opposite from Colleen's head. She and Bix crouched low, afraid to move, afraid to make a sound. All he had to do was peer over one of the boxes and he would see them there. Instead he ambled along to the end of the row of shelves. Colleen saw his elbow appear in her aisle. Then his shoulder. Then his pale blue eyes.

"There she is," he said with a grin. "There's my little playmate."

Bix stumbled backward but Heath was quicker, darting into the narrow space between the shelves and yanking Colleen up by the hair with one hand. With the other, he gripped her throat under her chin and dragged her out into the open space.

"Here's what I want."

Bix swore and lurched forward but Heath yanked Colleen back.

"Now, now. Everyone behave. You, too, Patrick." He spun Colleen around to see her husband, crimson-faced and aiming the gun directly at her. "I can crush her throat before you get a shot off. I'll do it. Don't believe me? Ask your wife."

Colleen saw black stars blossoming before her eyes as Heath pressed against the pulse points on her throat. How familiar this all felt, that longing to pass out, to miss another encounter with Heath. Bix and John were screaming at each other but Colleen couldn't hear anything over the roar of blood in her ears and Heath's quick rabbit breaths warming her cheeks.

Mostly she remembered that strange paralysis that weighed down her arms. She wasn't going to fight back. She was going to take it, whatever it was.

Finally Patrick's booming voice broke through her fog.

"What the fuck is happening here?"

Heath laughed and the sound of it ricocheted through Colleen's body. "It's very simple. John and I made a deal. He doesn't want to go to prison for killing that little girl dozing away in my trunk. I want Colleen."

Colleen groaned as she felt his fingers loosen on her throat long enough for the blood to come rushing back in. She knew how long he could make this last.

"Don't worry, Patrick. I don't want to keep Colleen. I just want her for a little while. An hour. Hell, probably not that long. I just charged my damn phone, but still, the camera's such a power suck." He bit down hard on her ear and Colleen cried out.

Patrick turned to John. "You agreed to this?"

"He agreed to a lot more than that, Pat. Didn't you, John?" John looked away as Heath tightened his grip on her throat and let his free hand slide down between her legs. He grabbed Colleen by the crotch and yanked her onto her toes. "One hour, one alibi—that was the deal. If our Colleen got stupid and went to the cops, John would swear I'd been with him the whole time, swear that either she was just being a vindictive, lying bitch or"—he squeezed his hand between her legs—"that she was just out getting her dirty kicks with someone else and trying to blame me. It would have been enough, Patrick, but then you decided you had to rough me up, you brute, you. That's when I told John he had to get his dick wet right along with me. Sweeten the pot, so to speak."

"You son of a bitch!" Bix screamed. It took a moment for Colleen to realize she was yelling at John. "You want to fuck her?"

"No!" John yelled back. "I don't want to fuck her. I just don't want us to be fucked. Come on, Pat. It's the only way."

Patrick's eyes were wide and white in his red face. "You . . . traded my wife?"

"Come on, man, he's not going to kill her. He's just gonna, you know . . . She's not the fucking Virgin Mary. You've seen the video."

Colleen felt blackness encroaching as Heath released her crotch and let her drop down into the grip on her throat.

"Yeah." Heath's breath was hot on her cheek. "That's what you get, hard guy, for making bad decisions, for losing that temper, for being born on the wrong side of the tracks. Now we can stand here all night. I know Colleen loves it, don't you, babe?" He bit her ear again, harder. "But I've got a girl dying in my trunk and you both need her alive. So what do you say we leave this up to Colleen? Huh?"

He released the grip on her throat and Colleen nearly stumbled from the head rush. "Sweetheart, here's where you get to decide. All you have to do is leave with me, and poor little foster girl gets to live. It's not that hard to decide. Pussy or death. It's not like you haven't given it up to me before. Come with me for an hour or that poor little girl dies."

Bix spoke up. "How do we know you won't kill Colleen?"

"Oh I would never kill Colleen. What would be the point of that? I want her to live with this. More importantly, I want her husband to live with this. I want to see how hard that hard guy is when he sees what I can do." He licked a wet stripe along Colleen's cheek. "You tell that big, handsome husband of yours to set that gun down and kick it away. You walk out of here with me, and you save that girl's life. And once I'm sure everyone's playing nice, I'll make sure your hubby doesn't do any jail time for his other bad decisions. Seems like a small price to pay for a dance you know all the steps to." He licked her cheek again. "Say yes, Colleen."

She wanted to say no. She wanted to die. She wanted Heath to break her neck once and for all, but she knew he never would. He would let her live just so he could enjoy the pain he had brought down onto her. She looked at Patrick, whose anger had faded to an ashen shock. His eyes were wet and his mouth hung open.

She wished she hadn't looked at him. She knew he would look at her like that forever.

Was her dignity worth more than a human life? Was her marriage?

She closed her eyes and nodded. She heard the gun clatter to the floor.

Heath pressed up tight behind her, grinding into her as he pushed her forward, whispering in her ear, "We're going to finish what we started, Colleen. There aren't even words for the things I'm going to do to you."

She stopped listening. She didn't hear his words. She didn't hear the shout behind her. She only barely felt the impact of his body crashing into hers as she fell forward onto the hangar floor. Instinct drove her to flip over onto her back to see Patrick standing over her, a wrench swung back high overhead sent crashing down into Heath's skull, once, twice, until John tackled him to the ground.

"The fuck are you doing?" John screamed.

The two men wrestled beside her, Patrick beating on John, John struggling to deflect the blows. Colleen scrambled to escape the arms and fists and feet, only to slide in the blood that puddled up beneath Heath's ruined skull.

"Get off of him!" Bix screamed. The two men continued to fight until a gunshot rang out.

Bix had picked up Patrick's gun and now stood over them, pointing the gun at Patrick. Patrick rolled off of John and the two men looked up at her, struggling for breath.

Bix looked pissed. "Somebody had better start talking right now."

CHAPTER TWENTY-ONE

"Bix, stop." John sat up. "There's no point in a gun. We're all going to jail. Thanks to Pat, we're all going to jail."

"Thanks to me?" Patrick said, sitting up beside him. "You're the one who—"

"Don't start, you two! Why are we going to jail?" Bix asked. "I want answers. Both of you, get up and get your shit together. Colleen, get over here." Everyone obeyed. Colleen stepped past Patrick, who staggered where he stood. She wanted to touch him, to take his hand, but couldn't seem to make her body obey her. Instead, she moved to stand by Bix.

Bix pointed the gun at John. "Okay. First things first. Someone had better explain to me why we are all putting our lives on the line for Ziggy Napier. Can someone tell me that? Because unless it's about a shit ton of money, I'm going to start shooting balls off."

Patrick cleared his throat. "One-point-two million," he all but whispered.

Her mouth dropped open. "Dollars? One-point-two million dollars for Ziggy? You're getting seven figures for a piece of ass? What the fuck does she do with that pussy? Spin gold and queef rubies? Who the hell would pay one-point-two million dollars to fuck a kid? God damn, I'll blow them and all their ponies for half that."

She pointed the gun at Patrick. "You got to tell me, Pat. What kind of deal is this? Who are you pimping her to?"

"He's not pimping her, Bix," John said, keeping his eye on the gun. "He's selling her."

"What's the difference?"

Patrick stared at his feet. "Shut up, John."

"No, don't shut up." Bix pointed the gun at her husband. "You tell me how that little piece of trash is worth one-point-two million dollars."

John stared at his best friend. "You tell her, Patrick. Tell her what the arrangement is with Arlen Henderschott."

"Shut your mouth!"

"Tell her what those asshole billionaires are buying, Pat! Tell her what the money is for!"

"Shut your fucking mouth!" Patrick screamed into John's face. Bix watched, looking more excited than afraid.

When Patrick said nothing else, John answered for him. "They're going to harvest her organs. How many of them did you sell? If you're getting over a million, I'm going to guess you sold her heart, both kidneys. What else? Her liver? Corneas? Skin?"

"You started this!" Patrick yelled. "Don't act all holy to me. You set up Amber Beth Cains."

"She lived, Patrick. She lived, and she volunteered."

"Like she knew what she was volunteering for. Like you really walked her through the risks. She was a freaking kid, John. You set her up. She thought it'd be like getting her wisdom teeth out. You brokered the deal to sell her fucking kidney, then you took your money and never gave her another thought."

"She lived," John said. "I was wrong. I know that, but she was desperate and so was I. So were you, remember? We were stupid to trust Arlen Henderschott, but we did and she lived. She more than lived—she got out, she's doing great."

"No thanks to you. I'm the only one who checked on her. I'm the only one who cared about her, who made sure she came through it okay."

John nodded. "You're right. You're right. I was a shit. It was illegal and it was wrong and I'm sorry I took part in it. But this? When Arlen pitched the idea of the ledger? Of taking payments to keep kids in reserve like some kind of takeout menu? Are you kidding me?"

Patrick hung his head.

"I thought it was a scam," John said with a laugh. "A con. Arlen and his rich-prick investors wanted to guarantee that their new little secret business could supply organs to other pricks too rich to sit on some list behind common people. They gave their money to Arlen Henderschott and we gave him access to Green Fields. Tested every kid that came through, keeping track of who might be a match with any of those rich douche bags."

Patrick whispered, "Shut up."

John shook his head. "We took in some pretty decent money in the beginning. And yeah, part of it was to pay off my little indiscretion, but then that cash just kept rolling in, didn't it? Such easy money that we thought we'd never have to cash in on. Figured we could just keep putting them off, telling them we were still looking for a match. What happened, Pat? Did someone get impatient? A friend of Arlen's get sick of dialysis?"

"An investor's granddaughter," Patrick answered, his tone flat. "She needs a heart."

"Oh." John nodded. "And then what? Arlen figured he was taking Ziggy's heart, he might as well find homes for the rest of her?"

"She was going to be dead anyway."

"Do you hear yourself, Pat?" John asked. "She's a kid."

"So is the little girl getting the heart."

"So her life is worth more than Ziggy's? Why? Because she's rich?"

"Ziggy is an addict!"

"Ziggy is fifteen!"

Patrick glared at him. "You've fucked younger girls."

John's hands went back up onto his head. Exasperation. Disbelief.

"Well now, hold on. Hold on." Bix cut them off. Her eyes glittered and her face shone with sweat, or maybe excitement. Colleen couldn't tell from where she stood, frozen and cold, stiff with fear. "I think it might be a little late for us to get up on our moral high horses. I mean, we've got one dead guy right here. Arlen Henderschott isn't just going to ignore that."

This couldn't be going the way it sounded.

"I'm just saying." Bix swung the gun back and forth between them. "How much money are we talking about? Long-term? What's our cut? How many names are on that list?"

"Bix," John said, "don't even kid about this. We're not doing it. This isn't running pills. This is murder."

Bix pointed to Heath's bloody body. "So is that. And that's already done. And I think we should stop pretending that any of us believe that's never happened before."

Patrick's face flushed even darker. He looked like he would explode but it was John who snapped first.

"Have you all lost your minds? Did you not hear what Heath said? Arlen has files on us. He has proof that we sold those kidneys. He'll have proof that we ran this deal. He will own us!"

"All the more reason not to fuck this deal up," Bix said. "We can cover up Heath's death. There are a million ways a piece of shit like that dies, but Arlen Henderschott is not going to take kindly to us fucking up a seven-figure deal. I wish you boys had come to me with this," Bix said, as if this were business as usual. "You know neither one of you all can find your dicks without me pointing to your zippers. Now the first thing we need to do is get Ziggy in here. She's no good to anyone dead in Heath's trunk. John, fish his keys out of his pocket."

"This can't work, Bix. It won't," John said. "We're not doing this."

"We have one-point-two million dollars for one kid and we got dozens of kids coming through here every month." Bix smiled at him. "This can work. Now, I don't give a shit about some billionaire getting a new colon, but I know for a fact that some of these little fuckers at Green Fields aren't going to live long enough to justify the money we spend on their laundry."

Patrick shook his head. "No, John is right. We can't do this."

"We can."

John laughed a hard laugh. "Let go of the fucking gun, Bix. We're not doing it. End of story. You waving a gun around isn't going to change that. What are you going to do? Shoot us?" He laughed again. "We're not going to do it and you can't do anything about it."

"You shut your mouth, John."

But he kept smiling. "No can do, Beatrice. You need us, and we're not helping."

"He's right, Bix." Patrick spoke softly, not taunting her. He came forward and put his hand gently over the gun. "We're not doing it."

"Oh yeah?" Bix asked, her face red. "Who the fuck are you to be making decisions? I make the decisions around here. If you stupid motherfuckers had let me handle this, we'd already have the money and be—" She tried to wrench the gun from Patrick's hand.

A shot rang out.

John flew backward, a red stain blooming on his chest. He fell back against the covered plane. Patrick froze and Bix finished ripping the gun free of his hand, turning quickly to target him.

He started to move toward her.

"Don't do it, Pat. You know I will shoot you."

Colleen didn't think about the gun. She didn't think at all but dove to check on John. Bright red blood pumped out over his chest in thick waves and his eyes rolled back in his head. His breath sounded thin and wet. She didn't know what to do. Put pressure on the wound? Where was it in that sticky red mess? Blood was everywhere and it looked like John would collapse under the slightest pressure.

"Bix!" she said, looking up at her. "My god." Patrick kept his hands up. He looked from the gun to John to Colleen and back to Bix. "You can't do this. You've got to calm down."

Colleen looked back down, pressed her fingertips into the mess that was John's chest, knowing the effort was wasted. Knowing she had to move. She had to run. She had to help Patrick, but she couldn't move. This couldn't be happening.

Bix wasn't pretending to be calm anymore.

"YOU shot him!" She jabbed the gun at Patrick. "You stupid son of a bitch. You shot him and now you're going to make this right. I love him."

Colleen heard John's breath growing wetter and fainter. "We need an ambulance! Call the police! Bix, please. Calm down. We need help."

"Don't tell me to calm down!" she shrieked. "You have no idea about anything!" She fired wildly over Colleen's head. Colleen flinched, deafened by the noise, and when she could hear again, Bix was muttering, "I can fix this. God damn it, I'm the only one who understands anything around here. This isn't fair. This isn't fair." Her words disappeared in a sob, which morphed into that horrible keening sound Colleen had heard in her kitchen that afternoon.

Heef-heef-heef.

Patrick reached out to her. "Bix, Colleen is right. We need to call the police."

"Oh now you're going to put your faith in the law?" Bix sneered now, the gun steady in her hand as those emotional shifts kept on coming. "Why? Because you're humping that princess? Let me tell you something." She jabbed the gun at him again, a dangerous replacement for her long fingers. "You think Colleen is going to have your back? The first time any of this gets messy, the first hint that the police are suspicious, and she's gonna sell your ass up the river."

Bix waved the gun at Colleen, her accent thickening. "They ain't gonna touch her. Little Miss White Bread." She turned back to Patrick. "She saw you kill your best friend. You think she's gonna keep quiet about that?"

"What?" Colleen said, lifting her red fingers from John's chest. "Patrick didn't—"

Bix trained the gun on her. "You shut your fucking mouth." She kept the gun on Colleen and turned her face toward Patrick. "I'm doing this for you, Pat. I'm taking care of this for you, just like John would." Her tone was gentle, almost tender. "I'm going to take care of this just like John took care of you. In Inez. After you beat that old fucker to death."

Patrick's face went pale and Bix kept talking.

"Yeah, I know. John told me all about it. How he stole his daddy's car to come get you. How he helped you burn your clothes and wash off all the blood. How he lied to give you an alibi and made sure you were far away when they found the body."

Colleen could hear Patrick's shallow breath over John's fading sighs.

Bix whispered to Patrick like a lover. "John did that for you because he loved you. And I love you, too. So I'm going to take care of this just like John would."

When Patrick didn't move—she didn't think he even blinked—Colleen had to say something. "Patrick, John needs help. He needs it now."

Bix waggled the gun at her. "Oh that's easy for you to say, Colleen. Why not call the cops, huh? Now that Patrick has taken care of your little problem. You hear that, Pat? She let you kill that son of a bitch Heath for her. You didn't have to. He wasn't forcing her to go with him. She wanted to go. She's been playing you all along."

Her tone became weirdly sexual and Colleen watched Patrick lean into it.

"She's always acting like some pure little princess, but you know the truth."

"Bix," Colleen said, elbows deep in John's blood.

Bix ignored her. "John told me about that video she made with Heath. Told me it was obvious she liked it."

"Bix!"

But Bix and Patrick were in their own little world.

"Pat, you and I always were the only ones who had the balls to do what needed to be done. I am all you have left in this world. I am the only one you can trust, so you mind me, okay? I'm going to take care of everything like I always do, okay?"

Colleen held her breath, waiting for his protest, waiting for him to tell Bix how insane she sounded.

Instead, he nodded.

She nodded back, smiling grimly. "That's right. Now you owe me, Pat. Fair is fair." She aimed the gun at Colleen.

That was enough to get her moving. Colleen dropped John and dove across the floor, trying to make it behind a rack of tools to her left. A bullet whizzed behind her. Patrick yelled, Bix yelled, but Colleen didn't hear either of them. Instead, she ran hard for the open truck bay door.

Another bullet exploded off of something ahead of her and Colleen swerved, ducking behind a stack of pallets. The move took her deeper into the maze of the storage shelves, but the truck bay door was less than ten yards ahead. All she had to do was run.

Over the sound of her own fear, Colleen heard Bix screaming at Patrick.

"See? I told you that little bitch was going to run. She's going to the cops. She's going to put you away." Bix commanded him to find her, telling him what she would do if he didn't. Colleen couldn't tell and didn't care if the threats were for her or for Patrick. Right now all she could think of was getting through that open truck bay door.

A motor sounded and the door began to descend. Colleen pushed off and ran. She had plenty of room, plenty of time. Bix's aim had been shit so far. Her brain ran frantic calculations of distance and the diminishing space between door and floor. What she hadn't factored in to the calculations was the grit and grime of the hangar versus the smooth leather soles of her riding boots.

She hit an oil spot and slid, falling hard on her hip. Before she could regain her feet, another bullet ricocheted off something nearby, the metallic ping ringing just a fraction of a second after the report. And another. And another.

Colleen screamed, scrambling blindly for cover. A branding iron burned through her side as something spun her, dropping her to the floor. She kept her momentum, however, and rolled behind a tall stack of cartons.

She'd been shot. Her brain couldn't quite comprehend the meaning of that, or the hot, wet stain spreading along her side.

Run. Hide. Get away.

That's what her brain fixated on.

Run. Hide. Get away.

CHAPTER TWENTY-TWO

The truck bay door closed.

Colleen heard it make contact with the floor. She had wedged herself behind a row of canisters and the wall. If the truck doors were to her right, that meant that the office door was somewhere to her left, opposite the truck bays. If she could get in there, she could call the police and, hopefully, make it out the front door without Bix or Patrick seeing her.

"You find her, Patrick," Bix barked. "Find her right now."

Bright spots of pain shot up into her armpit when she moved but Colleen didn't think she'd suffered any serious damage. Heath Seaton had taught her what serious damage felt like.

Heath was dead. Patrick had beaten him to death like he had beaten his social worker. What would he do if he found her first? Colleen didn't feel optimistic about her odds surviving Bix—shooting John might have been an accident, but Bix seemed committed to seeing this through— but if Patrick turned on her, she was absolute toast.

"Don't you hurt her, Bix!" Patrick yelled. Thank god. She had only Bix to worry about. "If you find her first, you give her ass to me."

Oh well.

Colleen hustled as quietly as she could along the short wall of the hangar. Between the cavernous space and her own panicked breathing, she could only catch pieces of the conversation being shouted around her. It didn't surprise her that Bix was the loudest and the clearest.

"You just get hold of her. I'll take care of her. I'm going to take care of everything."

Colleen tried to judge their distance by their voices. Over a short stack of pallets, she saw that she had nearly reached the front wall. Risking a glance around a tall stack of cardboard boxes, she could see the knob of the metal and glass door of the office. It sat on the far end of a ten-foot expanse of bare wall. Moving through the shadows, Colleen was searching for a path to the office door with minimal exposure when something clattered nearby. Colleen ducked down next to a rack of spare tires.

Her car. She was hiding next to her own car. Strips of duct tape held the mirror Bix had repaired for her a hundred years ago.

That had been this afternoon. A wave of dizziness crashed over her.

This couldn't be happening.

She recognized that thought. She had been enslaved by that thought for most of her marriage to Heath. This couldn't be happening. This didn't happen to people like her. Violence wasn't a part of her life. This couldn't be happening.

She had a scar where her spleen had been removed to prove that it could. She had a hot, raw bullet wound on her side to remind her that, not only could violence happen, it was happening again.

Denial wasn't her friend. She had to get to that door.

Biting her lip against the tearing feeling of her sweater ripping away from her bloody side, Colleen straightened her legs and peeked out over the bumper into the shadows, trying to spot any movement. Nothing.

She slipped out, tiptoeing. It felt like long, slow minutes but she knew it was only seconds before she got her hands on the knob.

Locked.

She twisted the knob back and forth as if she would somehow find the strength to rip the door open but nothing changed.

"You got her?" Patrick yelled.

Colleen dove to the right, into the racks and pallets she remembered searching through this afternoon with Bix, then wove her way through the workings of the Macaroni Brothers Freight Company, full of equipment and tools and bundles she knew nothing about.

This was Patrick's world. And John's and Bix's. She didn't belong here. She sure as hell didn't want to die here.

Metal clattered and footsteps sounded all around her, echoing off the high metal roof, until it sounded like an army bore down on her. Her only hope was to make it all the way around the hangar, somehow evading both of them, until she could find the button that Bix had hit to close the garage door. Everything else needed a key and she was the only person without one.

To her right toward the side of the hangar where the plane was parked, Bix swore and Colleen saw flaps of tarp canvas moving. To her left, she knew Patrick had to be close. As enormous as it had felt, the hangar wasn't that big and, with Patrick and Bix on either side of her, it suddenly felt miniscule.

The closet.

It jutted out of the wall just a few feet to her right. This was the closet she had found when Bix had fixed her mirror. Did it have a lock? Was there anything inside she could use as a weapon? At the least she could just hide in its darkness. Metal scraped the floor behind her. Someone was searching through the racks very close to her.

Colleen slipped into the closet and closed the door.

No darkness.

It took her a second to realize the closet had no ceiling. The steel shelves bolted to the wall went up seven or eight feet, the walls holding them went up three or four feet above them, and then the little space opened up to reveal the metal hangar ceiling high above. Dim light from the hangar illuminated the little space.

This was good, Colleen told herself. She could barricade herself in here and then climb over the top walls, lower herself down, and slip out of the hangar.

How, she didn't know. She didn't dwell on the question of how she would climb down or how climbing around would change her odds of slipping past Bix. All she knew was that any plan felt better than panic. If the closet bought her ten extra seconds to think, she would take it.

A quick scan of the space and Colleen realized those seconds might be all the decision had gotten her. Although it was almost a dozen feet deep, the closet was narrow, barely six feet wide, and most of that was taken up by the open steel shelves. The shelves on the bottom left had a cardboard carton with a few grimy bottles of motor oil. Two shelves up, she found some pipe ends lying on rags. Those could be useful. She grabbed one of the longer pieces, about two feet long, three inches in diameter, with screw grooves on one end, an elbow joint on the other.

It felt good in her hands, heavy and serious. The elbow joint gave her a handle of sorts. She didn't know how much good a metal pipe would be against a gun but she'd have to work with it.

On the top shelf on the right, four cardboard cartons of some sort of receipt forms would provide her only hiding spot.

It didn't take long to inventory the rest of the closet. The motor oil. A box with the little metal bits and wires would do her no good.

This wasn't her world. She didn't know what all of these things were for.

But she had some ideas about how she could use them.

CHAPTER TWENTY-THREE

She clung to the shelf support with one hand. She felt dampness on her aching knees but she didn't know if it was blood from where she'd scrambled around earlier or from the steel wire cutting into them. Maybe the blood from the wound on her side had started to run down her leg. Maybe it wasn't even her blood. It wasn't important. She wouldn't be kneeling here long.

Her hands were dry and that's what mattered. She gripped the metal pipe, rotating her shoulder in the narrow space to be sure she had room to swing it when she needed to. It was just a matter of time until they found her. There wasn't that much space to search. She wondered which one of them would be coming through the door and then she figured that that didn't matter much anyway. What mattered was how fast they came at her.

Colleen gripped the pipe and waited.

The heavy-duty shelves were bolted to the walls, making it easy for Colleen to climb all the way to the top. She was crouched behind the boxes of computer forms. It wasn't much of a hiding place but she didn't have to stay hidden forever, just long enough to maintain the element of surprise. On the other side of the walls, she heard Bix and Patrick talking.

"It's her fault it's gone this far, Pat." Bix's accent sounded harsher than ever. "You remember that. She's the one who ran out on you. On us. She's the one threatening you with the cops, okay? I'm the one you listen to now, you understand? I can fix this, but you got to do what I tell you."

Colleen adjusted the grip on the pipe. She hoped Bix came through the door first. Warmth flowed into her hands at the thought of this thick pipe shutting the woman's big mouth once and for all. Then she could talk to Patrick, reason with him. She could calm him down and make him listen.

Had she heard John correctly? They were selling kids for organs?

Could someone like that be reasoned with?

"She's not a god damn mouse! Find her!" Bix screamed and something clattered. Then more silence. How was it that they had missed the closet? Maybe they each thought the other had checked it. Maybe her plan hadn't been so stupid.

The door opened.

Patrick.

Of course he would see her. The shelving was steel grating, the boxes weren't that big and she wasn't that small. Even then, it took him a second. She watched him look around, work his way up, scan the shelves up to eye level, then above it. His eyes were red, his cheeks blotchy, and his hair was damp with sweat. He gripped the doorframe with those large, scarred hands she loved so much. When he finally found her, their eyes locked.

Those were not the eyes of the man she had loved.

"Come down, Colleen."

"No."

"Talk to me."

"Okay. I'll stay up here. You talk."

His fingers whitened where they gripped the wood. His head dropped forward, swinging back and forth. When he looked up again, all she saw was rage.

"I ain't going to prison, Colleen. You can't turn on me."

Can't rhymed with *ain't*. It sounded so strange coming from him. He sounded even worse than Bix.

"Let me go, Patrick."

"I can't do that." *Cain't* again.

"Shooting John was an accident. It was Bix's fault. I saw it. I saw everything. We can talk to the police together."

"Yeah." She had never seen that sneer on his face before. "Then you gonna tell them all kinds of shit." So strange. *Shit* had so many syllables. He sounded nothing like her husband. "You just gonna cover your ass."

"Patrick, you don't have to do this."

"Yes, I do. 'Cause it's always gonna be there. Out there for everyone to see."

"No, Patrick. I told you. It was an accident, you shooting—"

"Not that." He shook his head violently. "The *video*, god damn it."

"What?"

"That filthy video you and him made. You fucking crawling around, begging for it. It's always gonna be out there, hanging over my head. I married a whore."

Colleen could only stare at him for a long moment. Then she found her words.

"Fuck you, Patrick."

"Get your ass down from there!"

She hadn't known who would find her first, but she had counted on this—false bargaining giving way to impatience, then rage. Patrick stormed forward, all arms and muscles, tall enough to grab her and rip her right off the shelves.

He never saw the oil.

Before she had climbed up the shelves, Colleen had dumped the motor oil onto the floor, squirting it so that it spread out in a slick all across the bottom of the closet. Patrick's feet slid out from under him, in opposite directions, and he clawed forward to grab the shelf to steady himself. It brought him close to her. He grabbed the shelf low enough to expose his head to her.

She didn't hesitate. She swung the pipe down across the side of his head. She swung like she was blasting out of the world's deepest sand trap.

Her angle wasn't great, and it was awkward, operating from her knees. She swung through, though, letting the heavy metal pipe do its awful work. Patrick's head snapped to the side at a gruesome angle. Blood exploded from his cheek and temple. His body whipped sideways as his shoes slid in the oil. All six foot four of him thudded to the cement floor.

The pipe continued its arc, slowed but not stopped by the bone and flesh in its path, and hit the metal shelf hard, shock vibrations barreling up its length and nearly rattling Colleen off the shelf. The pipe clattered to the floor beside her bleeding husband.

"Son of a bitch!"

At the sound of Bix, Colleen righted herself and realized that her bad situation had suddenly gotten much worse. The one person she might have reasoned with lay bleeding. She had dropped her only weapon and was stuck on the top shelf six feet in the air with nothing to defend herself with but cartons of computer paper.

Bix kicked back the closet door. Her eyes had found Patrick first, but didn't linger there long. "You little fucking bitch," she snarled up at Colleen. "I'm going to kill you."

That seemed pretty obvious to Colleen. Still, instinct kicked in and she tried to shield herself behind the cardboard boxes. The cartons were no more than a square foot each, bound in pairs by thick plastic straps. Feeling stupid and desperate, Colleen tipped the cartons, dragging them back by the straps along the shelves, blocking herself into the corner. Something kept catching on the grating. Colleen didn't want to look away from Bix over the tops of the boxes. She certainly didn't want to lose sight of that gun, but after two feet, the boxes in her left hand wouldn't move.

The little box of epoxy had gotten jammed in the grate.

Bix had thrown the glue into the closet after she had reattached her mirror. She had said they would hide it there and retrieve it later. Bix had promised to keep her secret. Bix had come through for her as a friend when she really needed it.

Bix. Always so helpful.

Cartons of paper and a tube of epoxy didn't add up to much protection against a gun, but they were all Colleen had. Maybe Bix would jump over Patrick and slide in the oil. Then maybe Colleen could drop a box of the heavy paper onto her head, or even just onto her back. Give her enough time to jump down from the shelves, jump over the oil, run for the door.

"Fuck you, Colleen."

"Bix, stop! Talk to me."

"Alright." It came out like *ah-ite*. She grinned. "What do you want to talk about? Getting our nails done? How hard it is to find good help?"

"Don't do this, please."

"Okay." Her grin grew. "How about I do this?"

Bix fired the gun.

In the little space, it sounded like cannons going off in her ears. Colleen ducked down behind the boxes. Some part of her knew this was stupid. Bix was firing a semiautomatic. Those bullets could probably tear through wood.

It turned out, they couldn't tear through paper.

Bix's aim was dead-on. She hit the cartons squarely, rapid fire, over and over again. The boxes slammed back into Colleen with each round, little shreds of burned confetti scattering out the front and down through the grating. Colleen screamed as the *bang-bang-bang* deafened her and the boxes hammered at the arms she had crossed against them to hold them back.

She thought she had gone deaf. Then she heard *click-click-click*.

The gun was empty.

Colleen touched the back of the unmarked cardboard as if it were a holy relic and peered over the stacks of cartons. Bix stood less than ten feet away, her arm still outstretched, her finger still pulling the trigger. They looked at each other then, neither believing what had just happened.

Seeing that no more bullets were coming, Colleen rose up onto the top of the boxes and looked down. The front of the cartons looked like a papier-mâché project gone horribly wrong. Deep holes riddled the cardboard, pink and green and white paper bleeding out like party streamers.

It looked like a miracle.

Bix seemed less inspired. She glared at Colleen and threw the gun down.

"I don't need a fucking gun to kill you, you stuck-up little cunt."

Colleen grabbed the strap of one of the box pairs and pulled it farther along the shelf. In her other hand, she gripped the tube of epoxy. She didn't have a plan. She didn't have a thought except that she needed to grab onto something. The strap in her right hand broke. A few slugs from a handgun would do that, she figured. The cardboard gave out from the assault and a small avalanche of triplicate computer forms cascaded toward Colleen.

Bix came up right behind it.

Bix had seen the oil that Patrick had slipped in and launched herself off of Patrick's chest up onto the shelves. The steel grates were heavy-duty, but the impact of the larger woman shook them, rattling the paper swamp until several folds at the end slid off the edge of the shelf, unfolding all the way to the floor.

Bix stood on the lowest shelf, gripping the top shelf with both hands. She slid along the length easily, her eyes never leaving Colleen. Colleen scooted back on her butt, pushing away from her, searching the closet for any way past her. She could try to jump to the other shelf but Bix would reach her. She was taller than Colleen and stronger.

"That's right, you pussy. I'm coming for you. What are you going to do? You gonna call your daddy to come save you? You white-bread little princess." She grabbed at Colleen's leg but Colleen kicked out, connecting with her shoulder. Bix let go with that arm and swung out from the shelf, taking away all of the impact of Colleen's boot.

"Huh-uh, sweetheart," Bix purred. "This ain't no sorority pillow fight. I'm gonna drag you off that shelf and beat the shit out of you. I'm gonna make it last."

Colleen kicked more paper off the shelf. It fluttered out, unfolding like a ribbon. Bix pushed it out of the way, shoving it in front of her so the paper unfolded between her hands where they gripped the shelf.

Colleen kicked again, the heel of her riding boot making contact above Bix's ear then sliding off into her hair. Bix had perfect positioning to dodge any move and when Colleen tried to draw her leg back, Bix wrapped her arm around it, yanked Colleen's boot up under her arm, and began to tug on her jeans.

Colleen screamed, kicking her leg, but it was trapped between Bix's arm and the shelf. She flailed back, trying to get a stronger hold on the grating, when she realized she was still holding the tube of epoxy. Before she could let it go, Bix yanked hard and Colleen slammed down onto her back, her head banging into the corner support.

She was screaming, her voice loud and alien in her head. Her free leg kicked and thrashed, as if it had a plan of its own, and Colleen could feel herself sliding toward Bix, toward the open space at the edge of the shelf.

Desperate for a distraction, she clawed the lid off the end of the epoxy and blasted out a stream of the black goo into Bix's face. It shot out inky black, like toothpaste from hell, and hit Bix in the forehead and eyes. The shock of it was enough to get her to release Colleen's leg from her armpit and Colleen pushed herself back smaller than ever into the corner of the shelf.

Bix pawed at the black goo with one hand, hanging on to the shelf with the other. She spit where it had spattered onto her lips and large sections of her hair tangled against her hand and wrist, gummed up with the epoxy.

She grinned at Colleen, the black glue like war paint on her face.

Then she laughed that big belly laugh that Colleen knew Bix only used when she was making a fool of someone, when Bix was feeling really mean. She held up her hand, shiny with the smeared glue, and wiped it off on the front of her shirt.

"You think I'm scared of getting sticky?" Another big belly laugh, as if this were the funniest thing she had ever heard. "You are a precious little flower, aren't you? Or were you hoping this would all burst into flames? That I would spontaneously combust, just like the box said I would?"

She thrust a sticky hand forward and Colleen kicked more of the paper at her. It stuck to her like flypaper, crinkling and unfolding, distracting her for only a second. It gave Colleen enough time to curl up smaller, to pull her legs up close to her chest, hopefully making it more difficult to pull her down.

Something dug into her pelvis. At first she thought it was more damage from the wound that continued to bleed, the wound she realized she had forgotten all about. Colleen dug her fingers into her jeans where she felt something poking her. Something small and hard. She dug it out of her pocket.

Bix's lighter.

Her fingers shook as she flipped the top of the lighter back. Bix saw it and an ugly series of expressions passed over her face. Then she went back to grinning.

"Go on, you little cunt. You don't have the fucking nerve."

Colleen had the nerve. She just didn't know if she had the dexterity. One flick, then two and Bix laughed that big laugh again. Bix had just succeeded in hauling herself up higher onto the shelf to grab her when the lighter ignited. Colleen threw it at Bix's face.

The epoxy box had warned that the product was extremely flammable.

That was an understatement.

The black goo didn't so much catch fire as become fire. Yellow flame blossomed everywhere the epoxy was. Unfortunately for Bix, she had smeared it in a thin coat over her face and hair, and in seconds, everything from the shoulders up erupted in flames.

Colleen could see her eyes widen in shock. An impossibly high-pitched scream tore from her as her lips blistered and blackened under the flecks of burning epoxy she had spit out. Colleen kicked back, just wanting to be away from this nightmarish sight, and computer paper splashed out from beneath her heel. It slid out toward the fire and ignited as well.

It took seconds for the fire to be everywhere on Bix, followed by thick black smoke. Colleen didn't know which of them screamed louder. Bix released the shelves to slap at the flames engulfing her head. She fell backward, hard against the shelves opposite them, and crumpled to the floor.

Her long fingers clawed at the flames, catching fire themselves as the epoxy spread and burned. Colleen could only stare at the horrible sight—Bix twisting and writhing, finally falling over onto her side.

Into the motor oil.

Flames shot up around her, yellow and blue and rippling across the surface of the oil toward the door. More paper streaming off the shelf caught fire as well, snapping Colleen from her shock. She scrambled over the shelf, mindless of the stabbing pain in her sides and knees.

All she could think was, out out out.

The sight of Patrick bleeding on the floor stopped her only for a second. The flames licked up the soles of his shoes, smoking at the cuffs of his pants. He didn't cough, he didn't wheeze. Was he dead? His oil-soaked pants and shirt ignited, brilliant with blue and yellow.

Colleen jumped from the shelf, clear of the oil, and ran for the truck bay doors.

Outside the immediate grip of the fire, Colleen felt disoriented. She ran forward, then turned left. She couldn't think. Noise. It took her several moments to realize that noise wasn't just in her head. The smoke detectors were going off, blaring to nobody.

Smoke billowed out from the chimney that was the closet and Colleen was thankful for the high ceilings of the hangar. She had to move, to get out. She had to calm down. Find the switch to open the truck bay doors. Out. Get out. The shrieking alarm made it difficult to think.

She felt as if she had run laps around the building, as if she had been running for hours, but she had only run to the center of the hangar. Ahead to the right stood the truck doors. She had to get out of the hangar before the smoke filled the space. Who knew what sort of explosives or flammables were stored in here? Besides the ones she had used to kill Bix, of course. And Patrick.

Her stomach rolled at that and she could feel herself getting dizzy. Her side burned where the bullet had grazed her. Black flowers blossomed in front of her eyes.

She needed to get the garage door open. Where was the switch? Did it need a code? Would she be smart enough to open it or was this like the mirror and the epoxy, something that she would never figure out?

A panel. A button. "Press to open."

Oh.

She slammed her palm against it, half expecting it to beep and ignore her, but a motor rumbled, the door vibrated, and then began to rise.

"Oh thank god," Colleen whispered, waiting for the door to lift. She gave it a foot and then scrambled beneath the edge. Car. Phone. Police. She could do this.

Headlights blinded her as soon as she straightened up. The police had already made it. Or the fire department. Of course, the alarm was probably linked, right? She raised her hands, waving blindly into the light.

She heard a car door open and Colleen ran toward the sound, hoping to be caught by a police officer or a firefighter, someone who would usher her out of the way, someone who would tell her everything was okay, that she was safe.

Instead she heard a voice. Deep, male, comforting.

"Colleen McElroy?"

"Yes! Yes! Help me!"

She ran forward, already relishing the thought of collapsing.

Then she saw the gun pointed at her.

"If you don't want a bullet in your brain, get into the car. Now."

Colleen did as she was told.

CHAPTER TWENTY-FOUR

Maybe it was shock. Maybe she had just lost too much blood to fight another fight. Maybe there just wasn't a better option. Whatever it was, Colleen found herself sitting in the back seat of a Lincoln Town Car, watching Lexington's evening traffic go by. She was sitting on a towel. Whoever these men were, they didn't want any blood on their seat. It seemed a reasonable request.

She was incredibly thirsty. Her ears still rang from the fire alarm. Her sweater clung to her side, stiff with blood. Her sinuses hurt as if they had been scrubbed with a brush. Colleen knew that discomfort was connected to the pain of her fingertips. All ten fingertips were red. Several had blisters. She would think about that later.

She put her head back against the seat and closed her eyes. When she opened them, she saw a sweeping circular driveway, wrought-iron lanterns, and a well-manicured flagstone path. This was where Arlen and Dilly lived. Colleen had been here several times when she was married to Heath. Heath had moved here after the divorce. Did he still live here?

Oh, no. Heath didn't live anywhere anymore.

The man opened the door for her. That was thoughtful. Climbing out of the low car awakened hot pain in her side and she felt something warm trickling down from her ribs. Her knees ached, her hands throbbed. Her eyes wanted to water but they were so dry.

"Come inside," Dilly said after opening the front door. "I'll get you a drink."

That sounded good.

Dilly Seaton Henderschott.

Colleen stopped midstep. A stupid thought smacked her in the face. That old expression *Out of the frying pan and into the fire.* What came after the fire?

Dilly Seaton Henderschott, apparently.

She followed her to a room at the back of the house—the library, she remembered Dilly calling it, although there were only a handful of books arranged high on its oak shelves. Colleen had always admired the lovely maroon Aubusson rug over the dark hardwood floor, the way it brought the whole room together. Low round game tables, high-backed wing chairs in mismatched fabrics, vases and sculptures and figurines, perfectly placed. Dilly had wonderful taste. Colleen's fingers traced the edge of an antique writing desk. She smelled smoke. Had Dilly started a fire in the fireplace? She glanced across the room at the massive stone fireplace. No. That smoke she smelled was on her.

Colleen closed her eyes and felt the room spin.

"Sit down, Colleen."

Dilly had taken the seat behind the writing desk. She looked like the boss of some company, which made Colleen . . . what? A secretary? Someone applying for a job? Something subordinate. "May I have a drink of water?"

"It's over there on the bar cart, just to your left." It wasn't until she gestured that Colleen realized Dilly was now holding a gun. Three guns in one day. Huh.

"Thank you." Colleen focused on the cushiony feeling of her feet sinking into the carpet. The pitcher of ice water was heavy but the cool handle felt good on her blistered fingertips. The wonderfully cold water hurt her throat and she made sure not to gulp. "Are you going to call the police?"

"Of course not. Why don't you sit down, Colleen?"

"It hurts to sit. I'm stiff."

"Alright. If it helps, please stand." Very gracious. She put the gun down on the desk. "Tell me what happened in the hangar. What was burning?"

"Bix Mulroney."

Dilly's eyes widened just a fraction, their pale blue irises fully exposed. Then her expression returned to normal, well, except for a little smile. "That sounds unpleasant."

"Why am I here?"

"Your husband called my husband. Said something had gone wrong. Something about the girl running away to the hangar. I wanted our men to be there to be sure nothing got out of hand. I wanted to be sure you got out safely."

Colleen thought about the man's threat to put a bullet in her brain. All things considered, it wasn't the worst thing to happen to her today. "Do you know what they were doing?"

"I know the basics."

"I'd like to call the police."

Dilly's smile widened. "Hmm, I can see why that would seem like a good idea at first blush. But tell me, Colleen. How would that look? Have you thought that through?"

No, Colleen hadn't thought anything through, had she? All day long, she had been the last to understand what was going on, always late to the party, always slow on the uptake. She sipped her water and said nothing.

"Do you really wish to see your husband led out in handcuffs? Taken to prison? All over some misunderstanding? Some foolish business deal? There will be charges neither of you are expecting—child pornography, sex trafficking, drugs. Safeguards have been put into place to ensure that Patrick upholds his professional obligations."

Colleen could see Patrick at her feet, bleeding, flames licking at his clothes. It felt like something she had seen in a magazine. She supposed at some point soon, that image would hurt.

Now it just felt like something she had seen in passing. "Why—" She cleared her throat, tasting blood and smoke. "Why did you pick me up?"

"Insurance. Patrick loves you. We would like to ensure that he doesn't suddenly become squeamish. You will tell him to continue the work."

"Why would I do that?"

"For a number of reasons." Dilly leaned back in the wooden chair, her knifelike bob points swinging as she moved. "You don't want to be known as the woman who married not one but two monstrous men. Yes, yes, I know I defended my brother when you two split up. I overlooked his lesser qualities, but I do understand that he was not an ideal husband."

Funny, Colleen thought, both of her husbands were dead. Tonight. She wondered if she should tell Dilly this, tell her that this leverage plan wouldn't work because neither man had survived this enterprise. Again the thought arose that this truth would really hurt once it sank in. There wasn't any point in bringing it up though, was there? Nobody ever listened to her anyway.

Colleen sipped her water and began to stroll through the room, listening to Dilly.

"It would be quite a scandal. Patrick would be accused of using his access to Green Fields to molest and traffic young girls and boys. You would be disgraced. That disgusting video would surface again."

Colleen stood in the center of the room, the stone fireplace before her, Dilly behind her. She believed that somehow Dilly could still see the expression on her face.

Dilly kept talking in that low, even tone. "Of course, nobody wishes to see that filth again. That sort of perversion was difficult to watch, made harder still by knowing it was committed by someone who had been granted the Seaton name, someone we had accepted into our family."

Colleen's fingers went to her throat, her pearls. They were still there. After all of this, those pearls were still there. She never took them off. Not anymore. Heath had taken them off, the last night of their marriage. He had taken them off and replaced them with a thick leather band that he yanked on. He used it to drag her around, to hold her down, to lift her battered face to the camera. He'd loosened the band enough to give her the air to make the sounds he wanted to hear.

Begging. Filth. Barking.

Sounds to please him enough to keep her alive.

No, Dilly, Colleen thought, we certainly wouldn't want that video to surface again.

Dilly sighed. "You were always such a child, Colleen. It's time for you to grow up."

Another sip and Colleen realized her glass was empty. She set it on a small leather-topped table inlaid with a marble chessboard with malachite chessmen. A beautiful piece. She made sure to place the glass on an inset coaster and continued her stroll around the room.

Dilly was still talking. This was more than she had ever spoken to Colleen during her marriage to Heath. "If you're unhappy with this business Patrick is working on, you could tell him to stop. There will be other opportunities. This is the world we live in—men of distinction waving their sticks around while the real power lies with us, the women they love. Patrick does love you; he's repeated it to the point of being tedious. He's also quite ambitious. Arlen is impressed with him. Are you listening to me?"

Colleen stopped by a mahogany pedestal table, just a few feet from Dilly and the writing desk. She had made a full circuit of the room while Dilly had talked and talked, her low tones fighting with the tinny ringing in Colleen's ears. Colleen ran her sore, burned fingertips over the tasteful objects displayed here, bringing them to rest on a small stone globe.

"This is lovely." She picked it up. It was heavy and cool as she turned it over in her palms. Continents of colorful stone were set into the orb—malachite for Africa, turquoise for South America, rose quartz for North America, something coppery for Asia. "It's heavy."

"That's a very fitting image, Colleen. What do they call that? A metaphor? You have the whole world in your hands." Dilly held out her hands as if giving Colleen the world as a gift. "Now it's time for you to learn how the world truly works. This isn't a little girl's storybook. This isn't a morality tale. I need to know if you truly understand how our world works and what your place in it is."

Colleen set down the globe. Her shoulders ached. She rolled them and heard cracking. Dilly continued to talk. How many words had Colleen heard today, she wondered? Millions, she'd bet. Her right shoulder loosened as she swung her arm. Dilly talked and Colleen thought about how many of those millions of words today had been about how little Colleen understood things—all sorts of things, like car mirrors, arguments between men, and why it was okay to sell children.

"What are you doing, Colleen?" Dilly sounded more irritated than concerned.

"My shoulders are stiff." She swung her right arm in wide circles, clockwise, then counterclockwise. "Bix shot at me. It just grazed me, but I'm getting very sore." Dilly scowled at her, then nodded. "Maybe

Arlen can take a look at it later on," Colleen suggested. "Keep the scar-ring to a minimum."

"Of course he will." Dilly relaxed and smiled. Colleen could see those small, white, even teeth that were so much like Heath's. "He'll see to it that the scar will be small. Of course, it doesn't really matter. Your bikini days are certainly behind you."

Colleen almost mentioned that her bikini days had ended with the long scar along her abdomen that Heath had left her with, but there didn't seem any point in bringing it up.

A cell phone chimed, something light and classical. Tasteful. Colleen knew it had to be Dilly's phone.

"Yes?" Dilly said, keeping her eyes on Colleen. As she listened, her hard expression morphed into something reptilian. She tightened her grip on the gun. "Keep me informed."

Colleen swung her arm. Clockwise. Counterclockwise.

Dilly stared at her. "It seems the situation at the hangar is worse than it appeared at first glance. Would you care to fill me in?"

Clockwise. Counterclockwise.

"Colleen, you understand that you are only here as a courtesy to Patrick McElroy. If something has happened to Patrick—"

Colleen cut her off.

"When I was at St. Agatha's, there was a sign that hung on the wall in Millory Hall in the most beautiful calligraphy." Clockwise. Counterclockwise. "I used to read it every day. I had forgotten it for a long time, but then an old friend from school reminded me of it. I remember how much I loved it." Colleen closed her eyes, thinking of Alyssa's laughter at her outrageous high school prank. The forgot-ten words came flooding back. "It said, 'For unless Conscience knows Truth, history is static. See Hope itself tremble.'"

Dilly cocked her head to the side. Funny, that's just how the headmistress had reacted. Beautiful words that sounded serious and profound, the kind of words a wise person should appreciate, the kind of words spoken by someone who understands how the world truly works.

A pompous obfuscation by a teenager with a message to the world:

Fuck this shit.

Dilly nodded sagely, just like Headmistress Concetta had. She stroked the gun with her thin fingers and nodded. "I like that. Personally, I like to live by the words of Andrew Carnegie, who said—"

Colleen didn't get to hear the words of Andrew Carnegie. On the downswing of her last, clockwise arm-swing, she palmed the small stone globe. It was about the size of a softball, but a lot heavier. Colleen took that into account as she delivered her pitch.

No seams to find. No time to cock it at her hip or complete a full windmill with it. Just stride and fire.

The heavy orb barely cleared the edge of the desk. It hit low. What the pitch lacked in precision, it made up for in mass, striking Dilly square in the right breast. It threw her back in her chair, knocking the wind out of her and tipping her back against the wall.

Colleen wasn't sixteen anymore. She wasn't a fit high school athlete going after a fat girl from Trinity High School. On the other hand, there was no umpire standing in her way. And there was a lot more at stake than a high school softball game.

Colleen roared over the desk, all teeth and fists and screams. She landed hard on Dilly, knocking the chair all the way to the ground. She fought with her knees and her elbows and her blistered fingertips. When Dilly clawed at her hair, Colleen brought her forehead down to smash into her nose. When Dilly snarled and bucked, Colleen jammed her thumbs deep into her mouth and gouged her fingers into her eye sockets until she had a grip on her cheekbones. Dilly bit down hard and Colleen used that grip to slam the other woman's head down against the ground, against the leg of the chair, against a picture frame that lay broken beneath her.

Again and again she pounded the woman's skull, ignoring the blood, mindless of the pain shooting through her body.

It took seconds. It took forever.

Dilly stopped moving. Colleen pulled her fingers out of the mess that had been her face. She heard the words she had been shouting over and over again.

"I am calling the police."

CHAPTER TWENTY-FIVE

Colleen looked down at her socks. Her legs were crossed at the ankle on top of the thin, tan hospital blanket. The nurse had elevated the head of her bed slightly, not enough to interfere with the gauze pad taped to her side. Her ruined sweater set lay in a plastic bag on the seat beside her, her filthy boots standing guard beneath the seat. She still wore her grimy jeans and bra. The nurse had given her a thin paper jacket to wear.

Little gold horses danced across her blue wool socks. They were the only thing touching her that looked undisturbed. She wiggled her toes and tried to remember where she'd gotten these socks. She decided to buy more of them.

It was the easiest thing to think about. An IV drip delivered saline and antibiotics into a right arm that had turned so many colors it didn't seem possible it belonged to her. Scratches, bruises, burns, stains—her body looked as if someone were projecting a war movie and using her for a screen. The slightest move slammed her back into reality.

Outside the door of her emergency room stall, the cop leaned against the wall, checking her phone, chatting with the nurses. Sergeant Manilla had introduced herself after the nurses had checked her in. None of Colleen's injuries were life-threatening so, despite her traumatic evening, she'd gotten in line with heart-attack victims, kids with broken arms, and food-poisoning sufferers. She had told the sergeant what she had told the paramedics and the cops on the scene and the nurse who had checked her in—that she wouldn't say a word until her attorney arrived.

The cop had just smiled. Manilla had to be in her early fifties, slim and calm. If her beat was the late-night emergency room beat, Colleen imagined it would be hard to rattle her. Manilla took her post in the doorway, waiting with a cop's patience. She was probably used to hearing long, crazy stories. Once Alyssa got here, this cop was going to hear a doozy.

Colleen caught bits of chatter from the hallway. Dilly had been brought in ahead of her. Critical, Colleen had heard. Good. There was more talk about accidents and gunshots and fires. She heard the words *burn unit* and wondered if Bix or Patrick had survived. Prayed Ziggy had been found.

What a horror. She shut her eyes at the thought of Patrick's beautiful face burned. The pain he would be in. The agony of recovery. The months of skin grafts.

Then she wondered if the doctors would solicit a donation from the Skin Bank and her pity evaporated.

On the TV near the door, show after show passed by, muted and frantic. A nurse had given Colleen the remote and she considered turning on the sound just to pass the time. The screen filled with an animated diagram demonstrating how to properly operate an air compressor. Colleen shut the set off. Someone else telling her how things worked.

She lay back and closed her eyes, listening to the muffled chaos of the emergency room. A familiar voice roused her from a dreamless sleep.

"Yes, thank you. I am Mrs. McElroy's attorney." Alyssa Rovito stood at the door, her messily elegant hair more messy than elegant at this hour. Sergeant Manilla waved her into the room. Alyssa shut the door and hurried to the bed, her eyes wide and worried. She brushed Colleen's hair off her forehead, her finger hovering over the bandages and bruises the fight with Dilly had brought.

"My god, Colleen," she whispered. "Tell me everything that happened. Are you okay? Do we need to talk about anything in private first before we go on record with the police?"

"We sure do."

"Okay," Alyssa said. "But there's business first. I brought you some clothes." She pulled up her enormous handbag and pulled out something soft. A pale yellow sweater twin set. Of course Alyssa would have one. Of course she would bring one for Colleen. She set the sweater on the bed and leaned over Colleen.

"Let me get these pearls off before something happens to them."

Colleen brought her bandaged fingers to her throat. "No. Leave them there. They're fine." The little pearls rolled beneath the bandages.

Alyssa nodded, her eyes soft. "Okay. Keep them on. Start talking."

Colleen told her everything. It came out in jagged pieces in no order: Bix shooting John, John's predilection for young girls, Amber Cains's sold kidney, Patrick's arrangement with Arlen Henderschott to harvest organs for cash, Heath's sick deal with John, the ledger. She ended with the ledger and where to find it on Patrick's iPad. She told Alyssa about the passcode and the significance of the numbers.

Alyssa didn't flinch or interrupt, but she did grow pale as Colleen spoke. When Colleen finished, she nodded.

"Okay, are you ready? It's time to talk with the police. Tell them everything, Colleen. I'll be right here with you every step of the way."

"This is just a statement, ma'am," the cop said when Alyssa called her into the room. She stood at the bedside with a clipboard case and pen. "As I told you earlier, you really don't need your lawyer here for this. We're just trying to sort out what happened. We just need a statement."

The late hour brought out more of Alyssa's New Jersey accent. "We appreciate that. My client wants to be sure her situation is clearly stated.

I want it on the record that she is making this statement while being treated for medical trauma. She is injured and—"

Manilla held up her hand to silence the attorney. "Ma'am, I just need the basics. Believe me, your client is going to have all kinds of chances to tell her story. Can we get started?"

Manilla clicked her pen noisily and then pulled out a digital recorder. "It seems like you have a lot to tell us, Mrs. McElroy. I want to make sure we get all the details. For the record."

Colleen nodded.

"Your name, please."

"Colleen McElroy."

That cop-patience smile again. "Ma'am, I need your full name—middle, maiden, everything. It's for the record."

Colleen cleared her throat, still tasting smoke and blood.

"For the record, my name is Colleen Rose, formerly Dooley, formerly Seaton, soon-to-be formerly McElroy, soon-to-be forever Dooley."

Manilla looked up, her pen hovering over the page. This time her smile looked a little more amused. "Any other names you want to throw in there?"

"Yeah," Colleen said, squeezing Alyssa's hand. "Mad Dog."

ACKNOWLEDGMENTS

It amazes me how generous people are with their knowledge, insight, and resources. Thanks to all of these people:

Joseph Rimer, who gave me enough information about general aviation for three books. I'll be back.

Mandy Wheeler and Ginny Adkins of the Ramey Estep Home in Rush, KY. Thank you, not only for your time and information, but for the good work you do.

Tia Fletcher Campbell, a Kentucky girl through and through, for helping with the Pike County info.

Mike Farrell, for getting me into the Keeneland Clubhouse. Sweet.

M. Lynne Squires, who got that gasket epoxy into my hands.

Amber Cains, Sarah Dooley, Carter Seaton, and Marie Manilla for giving me use of your names. Well, for not calling me on stealing them.

Reenie Keeley, for the insight into St. Timothy's School.

Alyssa Rovito, whose donation to St. James Grade School got her name into the book and gave my character someone to trust. That wasn't so bad, was it?

Johnny Shaw, who made me laugh so hard one night at the bar that I had to put his words in Bix's mouth. Those of you who know Johnny will probably be able to spot the phrase.

David Downing, your awesomeness is getting ridiculous.

Jacque Ben-Zekry and all the amazing people at Thomas & Mercer who keep treating me like a writer and a friend.

Christine Witthohn, you keep cracking that whip!

Hannah Buehler and Dan Janeck for your tireless comma-wrangling and clarity-keeping. God bless you.

My friends who came through for me big time on this one—Debra Burge, Christy Smith, Angela Jackson, Tenna Rusk. I'd be in trouble without you.

And finally, to my family and friends who rode out this hard year with me. Special shout out and bourbon shots to my sister Monica. High rollers, baby. K? Snort.

ABOUT THE AUTHOR

Photo © 2015 Toril Lavender

S.G. Redling is the author of more than a half-dozen novels. A Hoboken, New Jersey, native, Redling was raised in West Virginia. After graduating from Georgetown University and living in New York City and California, she resettled in West Virginia and launched a fifteen-year morning radio career. Now off the air, she still lives and writes in West Virginia, simultaneously pursuing obsessions with locavore dining, sustainable gardening, and international travel.